MAX CASSIDY

ESCAPE
FROM
SHADOW
ISLAND

MAX CASSIDY
ESCAPE
FROM
SHADOW
ISLAND

Paul Adam

WALDEN POND PRESS
An Imprint of HarperCollinsPublishers

MAX CASSIDY
ESCAPE
FROM
SHADOW
ISLAND

that had been chilled to just above freezing. Max had approximately half a minute to get out of the handcuffs and chains, rip open the sack, and escape from the tank—thirty seconds in which he could drown or freeze to death. It was pretty straightforward, really. Provided nothing went wrong . . .

The audience listened in absolute silence. Attentive faces stared up at him, eyes watching him expectantly. They'd already seen this tall, good-looking teenager escape from knotted ropes and a padlocked trunk, from a straitjacket and a reinforced-steel safe. They'd witnessed him disappear from a cabinet and somehow materialize in the back row of the auditorium. They'd gasped at feats of memory and mind reading that had left them baffled and hungry for more. But this final trick was something else altogether. Max was an experienced performer, a strong, athletic fourteen-year-old boy—the Half-Pint Houdini, as the press liked to call him—but surely this death-defying escape was going to be too much even for him to pull off.

Max asked for a volunteer to help him, and hands shot up around the theater. Every child had an arm in the air, shouting, "Me! Me!" clamoring to be heard.

Max selected a skinny, freckle-faced boy in the fifth

row of the stalls, who ran eagerly up the steps onto the stage.

"What's your name?" Max asked him.

"Sam."

"And how old are you, Sam?"

"I'm ten."

"Sam, I want you to do something. Will you make sure I'm not concealing any key or tool on my body?"

Max held out his arms. He'd swapped the dark suit and bow tie he'd been wearing earlier in his act for a skintight body suit that covered him from neck to ankles, leaving only his head, hands, and feet bare. Sam checked the cuffs of the body suit, then the neckline and the bottoms of the legs.

"Did you find anything?" Max said.

Sam shook his head.

"Would you check my feet now, to make sure there's nothing between my toes? And my hair—there's nothing hidden in my hair, is there?"

The boy inspected Max's feet and head. "No, there's nothing."

"Thanks, Sam. Stick around; I'm going to need you again shortly."

Max glanced sideways at Consuela, his stage assistant. She was standing close by, as usual, a tall, dark, exotic-looking woman in knee-length boots, black trousers, and a sparkly red blouse. Her jet-black hair was held back with a silver clasp, revealing earrings that were as big and gaudy as Christmas-tree decorations.

Consuela came forward carrying a pair of handcuffs. Max stuck out his wrists and she clipped the handcuffs around them. Max held up his arms so the audience could see that his wrists were secured together.

"Sam, would you check the handcuffs, please?" he asked. "Are they properly fastened?"

"Yes," Sam said, testing them.

"Consuela will give you the key. Will you keep it safe somewhere for me?"

Sam nodded and slid the key into the pocket of his jeans.

The metal chains came next—twenty feet of high-tensile steel so strong that you could dangle a bus from them. Consuela wrapped the chains around Max's whole body so that his arms were pinioned across his chest and his legs and ankles were virtually immobilized. The ends of the chains were brought around Max's waist and clamped together with a massive padlock. His shoulders bowed visibly under the weight of the metal.

"Sam," Max said, "would you check the chains and padlock, please?"

The boy did as he was asked, tugging hard to make sure they were secure.

Across the stage, meanwhile, a curtain had been pulled back to reveal a large glass-sided tank about thirteen feet square and six feet deep. It was full of water and looked like a massive tropical-fish tank—though a tropical fish wouldn't have lasted a millisecond in the water the tank contained. It had been cooled to the same temperature as the Arctic Ocean. It was so cold that the glass sides of the tank were beginning to frost, and a thin crust of ice had formed on the surface of the water.

The audience were on the edges of their seats now. They could all feel the tension in the atmosphere. It was like an electric charge running through the air, making their skin tingle, their hearts beat a little faster. Max was a gifted escapologist, but he was still only a teenager. Did he *really* know what he was doing?

Max could feel the tension too, see the worry in the faces of the people watching. This was a very risky trick, but he didn't let that unsettle him. The first rule of escapology was to stay calm. Max had had that drummed into him by his father from the first moment he'd started learning tricks. *Stay calm and never panic.* The human body could function in extreme conditions only if you had complete control over it. A few nerves, a few butterflies in the stomach were fine. They were good for keeping you alert, for making sure you concentrated. But if you ever allowed the nerves to turn to fear, that was the time to start worrying. When you were frightened, your emotions got the better of your mind; you lost control and made errors. And for Max, one tiny mistake could be fatal.

Consuela fetched a large canvas sack from the wings and spread out the open end on the floor so Max could shuffle onto it. His ankles were bound by the chain, but he could just manage to move a few inches at a time.

He turned his head, nodding toward two men who had suddenly appeared on a raised platform next to the water tank. They were wearing thick, insulated rubber diving suits.

"These two men," Max said, "are on standby in case of an emergency. If I'm not out in thirty seconds, they will come in and haul me out."

Consuela lifted up the sides of the sack over Max's head and pulled the drawstring tight. A hook on a wire descended from the gantry above the stage and

Consuela attached the sack to it. At the same time, a large clock—a giant stopwatch, really—was lowered into place over the tank. The clock had only one hand, a second hand that would be activated the moment the sack containing Max entered the water.

It was a clever psychological touch—focusing the audience's attention on the time factor, the thirty seconds ticking by as Max struggled to free himself from his bonds. It was already starting to work. People were leaning forward anxiously, their faces taut, their eyes staring at the sack as it was winched into the air. They all knew that this was a truly dangerous trick. Handcuffs and chains were one thing, ice-cold liquid quite another. You could cheat with locks, but there was no way of cheating with freezing water. Max had to hold his breath; he had to survive the cold. The sack swung into position over the tank, swaying on the end of the winch.

But inside it, things were not going according to plan.

By now, Max should already have had the handcuffs and chains off. He should have had them off before the sack even left the floor. There'd be no time once he was in the tank. The second he hit the water, he knew the cold would begin to paralyze him, making it impossible to tackle the locks. At all costs, he had to be free of his bonds before then.

But he couldn't get the key. He hadn't deceived his helpers or the audience. The spare key to the handcuffs and the padlock—the same key for both—wasn't hidden on his body. It was hidden *in* his body. Over the years, Max had perfected the art of regurgitation—of swallowing an object and then bringing it back up again at will. He could swallow something small—a key or a coin, for example—and then contract and control the muscles of his stomach and alimentary canal—the tube that ran from his mouth to his stomach—to recover the object. He'd done this trick many times in practice—he never attempted an escape in public unless he'd completed it successfully at least twenty times in private. But tonight, for some inexplicable reason, Max couldn't get the key up. He'd tried twice already and failed both times.

Max knew he had only a few seconds. Once he was underwater and holding his breath, he'd *never* get the key up from his stomach.

He was nervous, and getting more nervous. This shouldn't have been happening. He could do it. He *could*. So why wasn't it working? *Stay calm,* he said to himself. *Concentrate on your breathing. Slow it down. Slow your heartbeat, too. Don't panic, you can handle this.*

He closed his eyes, focusing on working the muscles in his throat and chest. He felt them contract, felt the familiar ripple of movement in his stomach. This was it. This was the way it always happened. The key would be coming up, squeezing through his alimentary canal toward his mouth. *Just ease it up. Slowly, take your time.*

But then suddenly, without any obvious reason, the contractions stopped. Max felt a tightness in his throat. He'd failed again. What should he do? The sack was about to be lowered into the water. He could call out to Consuela. Tell her to stop the winch. But he'd never aborted a trick before. If he did so now, his reputation would be shattered, his brief career terminated instantly. It would be all over at fourteen. He couldn't face such humiliation. But if he didn't pull out now, he consequently might be much worse off.

Fifteen feet below him, Consuela was watching the sack intently. There was a smile on her face. She was trying hard to maintain her pose as the confident, supportive assistant. But her eyes were worried, and inside she was feeling sick with fear. She knew Max could do this trick. She'd seen him succeed all those times in practice. But practice wasn't the same as performing. Once you were out there onstage in front of a thousand people, everything was different. Inevitably, you were tense, nervous. The whole thing became harder, and more hazardous. Silently, she began to pray for Max. *Please don't let anything happen to him. Get him through this. Please.*

The sack was directly over the center of the tank now. Every eye in the theater was fixed on it. Nobody blinked. They were all waiting. Consuela gave a nod to the crane operator in the gantry. The winch motor whirred again and slowly the sack began to descend toward the water.

Max felt the movement. He had time for one last try. *Concentrate. You know you can do it.* It was pitch dark in the sack, but he closed his eyes anyway. It helped him direct his willpower to those hidden muscles inside him. Mind over matter, that was all it was. Channeling your thoughts to one particular area of your body, beaming them in like a laser, making your muscles do exactly what you wanted them to. The mind was stronger than the body. It could overcome anything.

Deep inside him, the valve at the top of his stomach began to open. The muscles in the walls of the stomach started to contract, to expel the key he had swallowed. The sack was still descending, but Max had shut out all external sensations. He was aware of nothing except

10

those tiny muscular movements at the core of his body. The contractions were getting higher now. Max was finally controlling them, moving the key gradually up toward his mouth.

The bottom of the sack touched the surface of the water. Freezing liquid seeped in around Max's bare toes, but he hardly noticed. The key was coming up. He knew it. The water was above his knees now, creeping higher. The cold took his breath away, but he ignored the numbing pain. Then he was waist deep. The padlock was underwater. *Nearly there,* Max thought. *Just a few more inches.* The water flooded up over his chest. It was like a vice around him, crushing him in an icy embrace. His shoulders submerged. The water inched up his neck. Max coughed and suddenly the key was there in his mouth. He lifted his manacled hands and took the key in his fingers, then filled his lungs with air only a fraction of a second before the water closed over his head.

It was cold, colder than anything he'd ever experienced. Even in practice it had never felt so bad. In ideal conditions, Max could hold his breath for several minutes, but in water this cold, when his body was fighting not just to keep warm but to keep functioning at all, he would be lucky to last even sixty seconds.

11

He inserted the key into the lock. His fingers had stiffened so much he could barely move them. There was no feeling anywhere on his skin. The ice-cold liquid all around him had numbed the nerve ends. Max twisted the key. Nothing happened. Was the lock frozen? His heart gave a jolt. He felt a sickness in his stomach, a fear that was turning to panic. *Stay calm . . . concentrate,* he told himself again. He tried the key once more. . . . It turned. The lock clicked back and the handcuffs sprang open.

Max dropped the cuffs and moved the key to the padlock at his waist, fumbling for the keyhole. How long had he been underwater? Ten, fifteen seconds? He had to move fast. But moving fast was something he simply couldn't do; he was too cold.

In the auditorium, everyone was staring at the second hand of the clock ticking around, then at the sack in the bottom of the glass tank, then back at the clock. Many of the spectators, like Max, were holding their breath. It was so quiet you could hear the ripples lapping against the sides of the tank as Max struggled to free himself.

Consuela's eyes also flicked from the sack, to the clock, to the two divers waiting next to the tank, watching for her signal. Was Max going to make it? Twenty seconds had elapsed. In practice, he had always been out by now. How much longer should she give him? She didn't know what to do. If she acted too quickly, she'd ruin the trick. If she waited too long, it might be too late for Max. Twenty-five seconds . . . twenty-six . . .

Max found the keyhole. He slid in the key and turned it. The padlock snapped open the first time. He grabbed the chains and tore them away from his body. He couldn't take much more of the cold. A moment longer and his heart would stop beating. He reached up, searching for the ripcord to open the sack.

Twenty-eight seconds . . . twenty-nine . . . thirty. Consuela glanced at the clock. She couldn't bear the tension. She had to act. Thirty-one . . . *Act now.* She looked at the two divers, started to raise her arm. . . . But before she could give the signal, the sack suddenly tore open and Max burst out.

His head broke the surface of the water. He gulped in air and splashed to the edge of the tank, pulling himself up the steps and almost falling down onto the stage.

A huge roar, like a volcanic eruption, exploded around the theater. The audience leaped to their feet, shouting and cheering and waving their arms in the air.

Consuela rushed over to Max and wrapped a blanket over his shoulders. He drew it tightly around his whole body. He was shivering and exhausted—more drained than he would ever let the audience see. But he was also elated. Elated and relieved. He'd pulled it off. He winked at Consuela, then walked to the front of the stage and bowed, acknowledging the adulation and applause. In this business, there was a very thin line between life and death. He'd stayed on the right side of that line this time. But only just.

2

THERE WAS ANOTHER BLANKET WAITING FOR Max in his dressing room. He discarded the first, which was already cold and damp from the water dripping off his body, and wrapped the fresh blanket around himself, sitting close to the electric heater that Consuela had switched on to warm the room. He was still shivering, his teeth chattering like castanets.

Consuela was standing by the dressing table, boiling a kettle to make Max a mug of hot chocolate.

"What happened?" she asked, her English marked with a strong Spanish accent.

He looked at her innocently. "What do you mean?"

"Don't give me that, Max. I know you too well.

Something went wrong, didn't it?"

"How could you tell? I was inside a sack—you couldn't see me."

"You took too long, and I could sense it as well," Consuela said. "I don't know how, but I could. All this time we've worked together, you get a feeling for things like that. I just know when things aren't going right."

Max hunched forward over the heater. He ran a hand through his thick blond hair, then rubbed his face. His skin was still cold, but he could feel some sensation returning, feel the nerves recovering from their icy immersion.

"I couldn't get the key up," he told her. "It took me four attempts."

Consuela went still, the kettle frozen in midair over the mug of chocolate powder and milk. She stared at Max in horror. "*Four?* My God, it's worse than I thought. Max, that trick is too dangerous. I don't think you should do it again."

Max looked away across the dressing room, but he didn't reply.

"Max, don't pretend you didn't hear me."

"It worked, didn't it?" he said eventually.

"You could have died."

"I had it under control."

This wasn't just bravado. With the confidence, perhaps also the folly, of youth, he'd already begun to forget just how serious the situation had been. He'd blanked out the fear he'd felt—and in the sack, with the water creeping up his body, he had been genuinely frightened—and looked back on his failure to recover the key as a minor blip, an unimportant little setback that had posed no significant threat to his well-being.

Consuela handed him the mug of hot chocolate and he took a grateful sip, feeling the liquid thawing the ice he could still feel inside him. She stood over him, looking down with concerned eyes. "Max, we need to talk about this."

"Not now—I'm too tired."

"I don't want you to do that trick again. The risks are too great."

"There are always risks. I can handle them."

"Can you?"

"Of course. It won't happen again. It was a fluke. Next time, I'll get the key up first attempt."

"And if you don't?"

"I will, okay? I'll do some more practice on it."

"You're so stubborn," Consuela said. "Just like your father." She saw a cloud pass over Max's face and she touched him gently on the shoulder. "I'm sorry, I shouldn't have said that."

"My father would have been proud of me," answered Max, a hint of defiance in his voice.

"I know he would," Consuela said.

She pulled out another chair and sat down opposite him. "I worry about you, that's all. Someone has to look after you, Max. And that someone is me. Occasionally, you have to know when to stop, when to stand back and say, 'No, this isn't worth the risk.'"

"I know what I'm doing," Max said.

"You're young, you're still inexperienced. Maybe this is one trick you need to come back to when you're older."

"I'm telling you, it's not a problem," Max insisted. "Now, I think I'll have a shower."

Consuela sighed and stood up. "I know you hate taking advice," she said, "and I hope I never see it, but if you're not careful, the day will come when you find yourself in a situation you can't escape from."

Max thought about what Consuela had said as he took his shower, the jet of steaming hot water massaging his body, reviving him. He knew she was right about him being stubborn and not listening to advice, but taking risks was in his nature. More than that, it was in his blood. His father, Alexander Cassidy, had been a famous escapologist too. Under his stage name of Alexander the Great, he'd toured the world for two decades, performing his show to thousands of enraptured spectators.

Max, his only child, had been encouraged from an early age to follow in his father's footsteps. Some dads taught their sons how to kick a soccer ball or land a fish with a rod. Alexander Cassidy had taught his son how to pick locks and get out of handcuffs. He had taught him the physical skills that his job entailed, too—strength, suppleness, agility, breath control. When Max was only a few months old, his father had taken him to a swimming pool and literally thrown him in at the deep end. Max had no memory of it now, but his mother had recounted many times how she'd screamed in terror at the sight of her precious baby being tossed into the water. But babies have a natural buoyancy, as Alexander Cassidy knew. Max had sunk beneath the surface for a few seconds, then bobbed back up again immediately and floated on his back, gurgling happily at his watching parents.

Water was his element. He loved it, and Alexander had worked on that love, teaching his son to swim before he could walk, then training him to swim underwater to build up his lung capacity. Max could now swim two lengths of an Olympic-size pool without once surfacing for air. That was a hundred meters underwater. On dry land, in a resting position, Max could hold his breath for nearly three minutes.

His skill with locks was equally impressive. There wasn't a lock in existence that he couldn't break, given the right tools. He'd been doing it for years, with his father's encouragement. At four, Max could pick a simple padlock. At five, he could pick the lock on an average front door. By the age of six, he could get out of a pair of handcuffs in less than a minute, and by seven, he'd gotten that time down to under ten seconds.

When he was eight, showing the rebellious streak that was a fundamental part of his character, Max had picked the lock of the head teacher's office at his school one lunchtime, using a bobby pin he'd borrowed from one of the girls. He had then stolen the keys to the classrooms and gone around the school locking all the doors. With the keys missing, and no locksmith available, the whole school had been given the afternoon off. Suspicion had naturally fallen on Max, whose mastery of locks was already widely known. He'd eventually come clean and confessed, and his parents had been called in. Max had been threatened with expulsion if he ever did anything like that again. His mother had been livid, and his father appeared so too. But Alex Cassidy was secretly pleased that his son was showing such excellent prowess with a bobby pin.

Max was fascinated by escapology. He liked nothing better than being with his dad, watching and learning how things were done. At first, he simply copied the tricks that his father performed in his shows. Then, as he matured, he began to invent tricks of his own, modifying some of his father's ideas and making them unique to him.

He had started performing in private when he was ten, small shows for family and friends on weekends. His first public show—a low-key event in the basement of a pub—took place a year later. By the time he was twelve, he was doing a show a week at different venues around London and had soon acquired such a reputation as a rising star that the London Cabaret Club, the most prestigious venue in the city, hired him for a short season, billing him as "The Great Maximilian." The run had been such a hit that the club had invited him back for a second season a year later, for which Max had devised a whole series of new tricks to tantalize his audience. Some were relatively straightforward and safe; others, like the sack in the cold-water tank, much more dangerous.

Max was supremely sure of his own abilities. He had a self-confidence that bordered on arrogance, a self-confidence that had not been undermined by the evening's events. So one trick hadn't gone exactly as he'd planned. That wasn't a fault with the trick, it was a fault in its execution. He'd work at it—hard work was something Max had never avoided. He'd practice regurgitating objects, he'd build up his resistance to freezing water so that the next time he performed the trick—and he had every intention of doing it again— nothing would go wrong.

He turned off the shower and stepped out of the stall. He had the dressing room to himself—Consuela would be onstage supervising the packing away of the equipment Max used for his twice-weekly shows. He dried himself quickly with a towel and got dressed in jeans, a T-shirt, and a black sweatshirt. He was slipping on his sneakers when the door opened and a man came into the room.

Max glanced up. The man was tall and thin, with a dark complexion and a head of thick black hair. It was difficult to gauge his age, but Max put him somewhere in his fifties. He looked around the room, his eyes darting nervously into the corners, across to the shower stall and toilet.

"You are alone?" he asked. He opened the dressing-room door again and briefly peered out into the corridor. Then he closed the door and turned the key in the lock.

Max suddenly felt alarmed. He often had visitors after a show, but they were always vetted by the security guard at the stage door and accompanied to the dressing room by one of the stagehands. Max was something of a teenage celebrity. He had to be protected from over-enthusiastic fans and the assorted nutcases who were always hanging around outside the theater.

"Wait a minute," he said. "What are you doing? Who are you?"

"My name is Luis Lopez-Vega," the man told him.

He seemed on edge. His eyes were never still, and his hands fiddled compulsively with the buttons on his jacket. Max noticed the man's fingers. They were long and bony, and the index and middle fingers of his left hand were missing.

"What do you want?" asked Max. "Why did you lock the door?" He backed off a little, getting ready to defend himself if necessary.

The man seemed to sense Max's unease. He held up a reassuring hand.

"Please, you have nothing to fear. I come here as a

friend, I promise. All I want is to talk to you."

"Talk to me about what?"

"About your father."

"My *father*?"

Lopez-Vega licked his lips. He was breathing heavily. He ran the back of his hand across his forehead, wiping away a sheen of sweat. "It is hot in here," he said. "May I sit down?"

Max hesitated. He'd never seen Lopez-Vega before, but he didn't seem like a threat. He looked frail and ill. And he wanted to talk about Max's dad. Max was keen to find out what he had to say. He gestured to a chair. Lopez-Vega walked toward it slowly, with a pronounced limp. When Max looked at his gaunt, lined face, he saw a shadow of pain and suffering in his eyes.

"Are you all right?" Max asked. "Can I get you anything? A glass of water, maybe?"

"Yes, thank you. Water would be nice," said Lopez-Vega, lowering himself awkwardly onto the chair.

Max turned off the electric heater. He filled a glass with water and handed it to Lopez-Vega, who took a sip. "Thank you. I feel a little unwell this evening."

"Shall I call you a doctor?"

"A doctor?" A ghost of a smile flitted across the

man's face. "No, I have no need of a doctor."

He drank some more water, then put the glass down on the dressing table next to him. "I am sorry to trouble you," he said apologetically. "I know you must be tired. I enjoyed your show, by the way. You are a very talented young man."

"Thank you."

"You are as good as your father. I can offer you no higher compliment than that. He was the best."

Max stared at him intently. "You saw my father perform?"

"Two years ago. In Santo Domingo. That is where I come from."

"*Santo Domingo*? Then . . ."

"Yes, I saw his last show," Lopez–Vega said.

Alexander Cassidy had disappeared two years earlier, in the Central American country of Santo Domingo, where he'd gone to perform. His body had never been found, but there was circumstantial evidence to indicate that he'd been murdered. Max's mother, Helen, who'd accompanied his father on the trip, had been tried and convicted of Alexander's murder by a Santo Domingan court and sentenced to twenty years in prison. She'd served eighteen months in a jail there but had recently been transferred to a prison in England to complete the remainder of her sentence.

"Did you know him? Did you know my father?" Max said eagerly. "Did you speak to him?"

"It was a fine show," Lopez-Vega said. "What happened afterward was terrible. The case against your mother was ridiculous. In a civilized country, a less corrupt country than Santo Domingo, it would have been thrown out of court on the first day. But Santo Domingo, alas, is not a civilized country. It is a country where people, where judges, can be bought like coconuts in the marketplace."

"The judge was bribed?" Max asked.

"The police also. How else do you explain her conviction? She did not kill your father."

"I know," Max said. "I've always known it."

"Your father is—" Lopez-Vega broke off as a harsh, racking cough made his whole body shake. He took another sip of water.

Max looked at him anxiously. "Are you sure I can't get you a doctor?"

The man shook his head. He took a few deep breaths, the air wheezing through his lungs. "You must forgive me," he said. "I would have come sooner, only I have been . . ." He paused to take another long breath. "Let's just say I've been *away* for a time."

26

Max leaned toward Lopez-Vega. All the tiredness he'd felt earlier had suddenly fallen away. He was alert, full of hope. "You say my mother didn't kill my father. Do you know something that will clear her name, prove her innocence?"

Before Lopez-Vega could reply, there was a sharp knock on the dressing-room door and someone tried the handle. Lopez-Vega gave a violent start and turned to stare at it. There was fear in his eyes. "No one must know I am here," he whispered urgently to Max.

"Max?" came a voice from outside.

"It's all right," Max said quietly. "It's only Consuela."

"Max, are you okay?" Consuela asked through the door.

"I'm fine," Max called back.

"Can I come in?"

"One moment."

Lopez-Vega was on his feet, one hand gripping the back of his chair to steady himself. "Do not tell anyone about this," he murmured. "Not a word, you understand?"

"Max, what's going on?" Consuela was getting impatient outside.

"Just coming," he replied.

Lopez-Vega put his hand on Max's arm. "Your father

is not dead, Max," he said softly.

Max gaped at him. For a moment, he stopped breathing. He felt as if he'd been hit by a truck. "What do you mean? What're you talking about?" he whispered.

"We cannot talk here. Come to my hotel tomorrow evening, eight o'clock. The Rutland Hotel, near King's Cross station. Room twelve."

"But you can't go. How do you know Dad's not dead? How? You have to tell me."

The door handle rattled. "Max, let me in," Consuela called.

"Tell me!" Max said urgently, ignoring Consuela. "Where is he? What happened to him?"

"It is complicated, Max. I will explain tomorrow."

"But I need to know—"

"Tomorrow. We need more time. And I have something to give you."

Lopez-Vega unlocked the door and stepped out past Consuela.

"Why was the door locked?" she asked, coming into the dressing room. "Who was that?"

Max didn't reply. He felt breathless and his pulse was racing. His mind was in turmoil, reeling from what Lopez-Vega had said. His father wasn't dead? Was the man telling the truth? Was Alex Cassidy really still alive, or was this some horrible, malicious trick? For two long years Max had lived with the possibility that his father was gone forever. But now this stranger had shown up and turned everything on its head. It couldn't be true, could it? Max wanted desperately to believe what this man had told him, but he was wary. Who was this Luis Lopez-Vega? How did he know what had really happened to Max's father? Max needed some answers. And he needed them now.

He stepped out of the room and ran along the corridor to the stage door.

"There was a man here just now," he said to the security guard. "Tall, black hair."

"He just left," the guard replied. "I think he took a taxi."

Max whipped open the stage door and ran out. There was a group of fans clustered on the pavement.

"Max! Max!" they called.

Max ignored them. He looked up the darkened street. The taillights of a taxi were just disappearing around the corner.

3

TWO YEARS AGO MAX'S WHOLE LIFE HAD imploded—collapsed in on itself. He could remember every tiny detail of that time: the shock of losing both his parents, his father apparently dead and his mother shut away in prison.

His father had been invited to do a couple of shows in Santo Domingo and, because Max was going to be away for a week on a school trip to France, his mother had decided to accompany her husband. Normally, Helen stayed at home to look after Max, and only Consuela went with Alexander on his frequent trips abroad.

Max remembered the bus pulling in outside the

school on Friday evening, the children worn out after the long trip from France but excited to be home. They'd scrambled to their feet, peering out of the windows, searching for the faces of their parents in the crowd by the school gates. Max had been one of the last to get off, his face tanned from the French sun, a carrier bag clutched in his hand containing a box of chocolates and some cheese he'd bought as a present for his mum and dad. He'd stood on the pavement, his classmates thronging around him, the luggage being unloaded from the hold of the bus, wondering where his mother was. He'd felt disappointed, maybe a little angry. All the other parents were there on time.

It was only when he saw the head teacher, Mrs. Williamson, approaching him with a uniformed female police officer beside her that Max realized something had happened—something serious, though he never imagined then that it would be quite as traumatic as it turned out to be.

They didn't give him the full story all at once. The policewoman took him home, told him there'd been an "incident" in Santo Domingo and his mother was going to have to stay there for a few days to sort it out. She had asked him if he had any relatives nearby who he could stay with, but Max didn't have any extended family. His mother and father were both only children. There were no uncles or aunts or cousins, and his grandparents were all dead. The Cassidy family consisted of just three people—Max, his mum, and his dad.

"What's going on?" Max asked. "What's this 'incident' you mentioned?"

"It's complicated," the policewoman said vaguely. "We're still not sure exactly what's happened."

"But my mum and dad are okay, aren't they?"

She didn't reply. She asked him about his friends instead. Was there someone whose family could look after him for the weekend? Max suggested his best mate, Andy Sewell, and went there for a couple of days. He was distraught, sick with worry. What had happened in Santo Domingo? Why hadn't his mum and dad come home? He tried to phone them, tried to contact them, but couldn't get through and no one would tell him anything.

Then, on Monday afternoon, Consuela turned up at school, having flown back from Santo Domingo alone, and took Max home.

Consuela Navarra had been Alexander Cassidy's assistant since Max was a baby. Max regarded her as part of the family, as the aunt he didn't have. She worked with his father, but she was more than just his assistant. She came for meals with Max and his parents, babysat when Helen and Alexander went out together, helped at Max's birthday parties, and bought him presents. There was a real affection between Max and her, and Consuela wasn't afraid to show it.

The moment they were alone, she put her arms around him and hugged him tight. When she pulled away, Max saw tears glistening in her eyes.

"What is it?" he asked. "It's Mum and Dad, isn't it? What's happened to them?"

Consuela told him everything. About his father disappearing, about his jacket and wallet being found on the beach, a blood-stained knife dropped nearby. At first, that's all it was—a mysterious disappearance. It was only several days later, after blood and fingerprint tests had been carried out and the locals questioned, that Max received the shocking news from Santo Domingo. His mother had been arrested and charged with her husband's murder. Three months later, she was convicted and sentenced to twenty years in prison.

With Helen locked away, Consuela had moved in to look after Max—to do the cooking and shopping as well as assisting him in his new stage act. The family court, with Helen's full approval, had made Consuela Max's legal guardian until his mother was released.

The months and years since then had been an extended nightmare for Max. He hoped daily that it would end—that his father would suddenly reappear, or evidence would be found to prove conclusively that his mother was innocent—but it didn't. It kept going, a torment that Max had learned to live with.

One thing he knew for sure from the very start: His mother did not kill his father. Such a thing was impossible, unthinkable. That knowledge, that certainty of his mother's innocence, was a comfort to him. At the beginning, he'd also felt sure that his father wasn't really dead. And although there hadn't been any sightings of Alexander or any other indications that he was still alive, his body had never been found, and Max hadn't given up hope. He had a powerful gut feeling that his father was out there somewhere, he didn't know where, and that one day he would find him.

Now this Luis Lopez-Vega had appeared out of nowhere, telling Max that his father was alive. Could Max believe him? After seeing his taxi driving away from the theater, Max wanted to hail another cab and go straight to the Rutland Hotel. But he stopped himself. It was late, Consuela would worry if he went off impulsively like that, and anyway, he needed time to think. He needed to mull over what Lopez-Vega had told him, try to make sense of it.

Max couldn't sleep that night. He lay awake, staring into the darkness, recalling everything the man had said. Max wanted desperately to believe that he had been telling the truth, but he also wanted to be cautious. If Lopez-Vega turned out to be lying, the disappointment would be unbearable.

At school the next day, Max struggled to focus on his lessons. His mind was preoccupied with the visitor from Santo Domingo, looking ahead to that evening's meeting. At the end of the afternoon, he walked home with Andy and a group of other friends.

His family circumstances were unusual, to say the least, and he had a blossoming career as an escapologist, but in most other ways Max was still an ordinary fourteen-year-old schoolboy. He enjoyed what lots of other teenagers enjoyed—playing soccer and computer games, listening to music, and hanging out with his mates. When he had the time, that is. Escapology was a demanding occupation that ate into his evenings and weekends. He only did two performances a week for three months of the year, but practicing was a daily routine that couldn't be avoided.

When he got home from school, he sat in the kitchen with Consuela for ten minutes, eating a snack and chatting to her about his day, before going upstairs to do his homework. But he couldn't concentrate on math and French, so he changed into his tracksuit and sneakers and went out for a jog, hoping that the physical activity would take his mind off his father and Luis Lopez-Vega.

Back at the house after his mile and a half around the local park, he went down into the basement, where his dad had set up a small gymnasium and practice area. There were exercise machines and weight-training equipment at one end of the room, and at the other were various trunks and cabinets identical to the ones Max used onstage. Suspended from hooks on the walls was an array of chains, manacles, locks, and handcuffs that made the place look like a medieval torture chamber.

Max took down a selection of the more complicated locks and practiced picking them with various tools—a screwdriver, a nail file, a piece of wire. It was all about technique and dexterity. And practice. You could have all the skill in the world, but if you didn't work at it regularly, that skill would disappear. Next, he took the key to a set of handcuffs and swallowed it. He was determined not to let the failure of the previous evening shake his confidence. Regurgitation was an important part of his act. He'd never had any trouble with it before, and he wasn't going to start now. He closed his eyes, imagining the muscles of his stomach and alimentary canal, tensing each set in turn to bring the key back up. And there it was in his mouth. First time, no problem. So why hadn't he managed it first time yesterday? Nerves, it had to be nerves. That was the only possible explanation. Max swallowed the key again, and brought it back up again without difficulty. He did it a third time successfully and felt any remaining anxiety about the water-tank trick vanish. He knew he could do it without a hitch next time.

To finish off the training session, he did more work on his physical fitness—a vital element in any escapologist's act. You had to be strong, you had to be supple, to be able to control your muscles, your breathing. The strain on the body was so great that if you weren't in absolutely peak condition, you could do yourself a serious injury, or worse.

He did a few stretching exercises on the gym mat, then ten minutes on the rowing machine, ten minutes on the step machine, and a further ten minutes lifting weights. By now, he was tired and sweating freely. He went upstairs, took a shower, and came back down to the kitchen for dinner.

Consuela was a good cook, with a fondness for the cuisine of her homeland—paella, fish, and lots of garlic and olive oil. This evening, she'd made chicken and rice, the chicken hot and spicy, smothered in a tomato and pepper sauce. Max ate greedily, one eye on the clock. He didn't have time to linger if he was going to get to the Rutland Hotel by eight o'clock. He hadn't told Consuela about his appointment. Max usually told her everything, but he respected Lopez-Vega's instruction to keep it secret. Max could feel the tension in his stomach, a mixture of nerves and excitement. "I'm just going round to Andy's for a game of snooker," Max said casually. "I shouldn't be back too late."

"Okay," Consuela said. "I won't lock up. See you later."

Max grabbed his jacket from a hook in the hall and went out. He didn't like lying to Consuela, but he didn't want her worrying about him. He was old enough now to take care of himself.

He took the Underground to King's Cross and then walked the last half mile to the Rutland Hotel. This wasn't an area of London he knew well, and it had a seedy, rundown feel to it. There were blocks of ugly flats in between the rows of terraced houses, trash dumped by the curb, litter blowing across the pavements. The Rutland Hotel was a high, narrow building squeezed in between a chip shop and a launderette. It looked cheap and not very inviting.

Max went inside. There was a small foyer with a reception desk at one end and keys hanging from a rack on the wall. An unpleasant smell, a mixture of disinfectant and boiled cabbage, wafted in through an open door at the back of the foyer. There didn't appear to be anyone about. Max went to the desk and waited for a moment. "Hello?" he called.

There was no response. He could see that the key to room twelve was missing from the rack. Lopez-Vega was here, and expecting him. Max climbed the stairs. There was an elevator, but he always avoided them. Being locked up in a trunk as part of his act didn't bother him, but strangely, elevators made him nervous. He had no control over them, he was at the mercy of a motor that might go wrong, and he found that worrying.

Room twelve was on the fourth floor, down a dark, narrow corridor at the rear of the building. Max approached the door and was lifting his hand to knock when he noticed that the door was slightly ajar. Then he spotted the lock. The wood around it was splintered, as if the door had been broken open. Max felt a shiver run down his spine. His common sense told him to walk away now, but he had to know what Lopez-Vega knew about his father. He pushed open the door with his toe.

"Mr. Lopez-Vega? It's me, Max." Max stepped into the room.

Max looked around the room, taking in the grubby wallpaper, the tatty furniture, the open suitcase and piles of clothes on the bed. It was only when he dropped his eyes a fraction that he saw the figure on the carpet, half hidden behind the bed.

"Mr. Lopez-Vega?"

Max edged closer. Lopez-Vega was sprawled on his back, one arm flung out to the side, his eyes and mouth gaping open. In the center of his forehead was a bullet hole; around him was a pool of blood.

Max turned away quickly, almost gagging. He hurried into the bathroom and leaned over the basin for a time, breathing in and out deeply until the nausea passed. He was in a state of shock. He'd never seen a dead body before, let alone one with a gunshot wound to the head. He tried to obliterate the image from his mind, but he kept seeing the blood and Lopez-Vega's blank eyes staring up at him, his mouth contorted into a silent scream.

He had to do something. He couldn't stay in the bathroom all night. Max cupped his hands under the tap and drank some water, then steeled himself and went back out into the bedroom, glancing briefly at the body on the floor again. How long had Lopez-Vega been dead? The blood around his head hadn't congealed yet. It still looked shiny and wet. Max knew that meant the killing had been recent, maybe only a few minutes before he'd come upstairs. And he suddenly realized—the killer might even still be in the hotel.

Max spun round. But there was no one there. *Come on, Max, calm down. Think,* he said to himself. *What are you going to do?* Well, that was obvious. Go back down to the reception desk and ask someone to phone the police. But he hesitated. Those clothes strewn across the bed—it looked as if Lopez-Vega had unpacked in a hurry. Or as if someone had been searching for something. Lopez-Vega had said he had something to give Max. But what? Had the killer also been looking for it? Had he found it and taken it away with him?

Max fingered the clothes—shirts, trousers, underwear—to see if anything was concealed beneath them. Then he rummaged carefully through the suitcase. He checked the drawers of the bedside table, too, but there was nothing inside except a Gideon Bible and a thick coating of dust. The wardrobe contained wire hangers and a spare blanket for the bed, but that was all. The bathroom was equally unrewarding. Just a couple of towels and Lopez-Vega's wash things on a shelf over the basin—toothbrush, toothpaste, comb, disposable razor, and canister of shaving foam.

Max was on edge, scared. He wanted to get this over with and leave. He returned to the body by the bed. Averting his eyes from Lopez-Vega's face, he concentrated on the rest of him. He was wearing the same light-gray suit and white shirt he'd worn at the theater the night before. It was a cheap-looking suit, with shiny patches on the trouser knees and frayed edges along the lapels of the jacket. The clothes confirmed what Max had already worked out from the choice of hotel. Lopez-Vega was not a rich man. Max couldn't bring himself to touch Lopez-Vega's hands, but he could see how rough and calloused the skin was. They were the hands of a man accustomed to manual labor, to working outdoors on the land.

Max took a deep breath and knelt down beside the body. He didn't want to do this—the very thought turned his stomach—but he had to know. Lopez-Vega had invited him there to give him something. Max had to find out if that something was still here. Carefully but quickly, not wanting to linger any longer than necessary, he went through the pockets of the dead man's suit. They were all empty. No wallet, no passport or money, not even a few coins or a handkerchief. The killer must have cleaned them out.

Max straightened up, bitterly disappointed. He'd never know now what Lopez-Vega had intended to give him or what information he had about his father. A sadness came over him. He'd met the man only once, knew nothing about him, yet his death touched him nonetheless. Who had done it? Why would anyone have wanted to kill this man?

Another icy tingle shot down Max's spine. His stomach fluttered. He suddenly sensed that he'd been in the room long enough. It was time to get out.

He turned toward the door—and out of the corner of his eye saw something he hadn't noticed before. There was something strange about Lopez-Vega's hair. Max made himself look more closely. The line of bangs across the top of the forehead had an odd, unnatural appearance—as if the hair had been torn out of the scalp. Max crouched down and touched the bangs. They were indeed raised clear of the skin, but it wasn't real hair. Lopez-Vega was wearing a wig.

Gingerly, Max peeled back the wig to reveal the scalp underneath. It seemed a horrible thing to do—taking the hair off a corpse. The skin of Lopez-Vega's head was smooth and shiny, devoid of even a single hair. Then Max saw it.

Taped to the underside of the wig was a small piece of paper about an inch square. Max unstuck the tape and lifted the paper off. Written on one side was a sequence of numbers:

11138352

That was all. No words, just eight numbers. Max knew the piece of paper was important. Why else was it concealed in such a strange place? He studied the numbers. What did they mean? Could this fragment of paper be what Lopez-Vega had wanted to give him?

Max slipped the paper into his pocket and went to the door, thinking again about what he should do next. Going downstairs and asking someone to phone the police no longer seemed such a good idea. He'd have to answer questions, explain what he was doing there. After what had happened to his mother, Max was suspicious of homicide investigations. It was a gut feeling, but he knew instinctively that it would be wise not to get involved, that in some way it would be dangerous to get mixed up in this.

He took out his handkerchief and wiped all the surfaces he'd touched to remove any fingerprints, then went out into the corridor. He couldn't expect the reception desk to still be unattended. If he went down the main stairs, he would almost certainly be seen and challenged. But there had to be a back way out. Hotels always had more than one exit.

There was another, smaller staircase at the far end of the corridor and an illuminated sign on the wall that read FIRE EXIT. Max headed toward it and went carefully down the stairs, pausing occasionally to listen for footsteps. He didn't want to bump into anyone coming up. He passed the third floor, then the second. As he neared the ground floor, he heard voices below him and stopped. He peered cautiously over the banister but couldn't see anyone. The voices came again, then the sound of metal scraping on metal, like a spoon in a pan. Max realized what it was—the noise of the hotel kitchen.

He kept going. At the bottom of the stairs, he stopped again and poked his head around the corner. The kitchen was to the right. Through the open door

Max could see a couple of sweaty-looking men in white aprons and caps cooking over a long range of gas burners. Next to the kitchen was an exit that led out into the backyard, a small, enclosed space with overflowing dustbins lined up along a wall and an open gateway to the street at the far side.

Max waited until the cooks had their backs toward him, then darted past the kitchen and out into the yard. He ran across it and through the gate onto the street, turning left and sprinting away from the hotel.

It was almost dark now. The streetlamps were on and the pavements were bathed in an eerie yellow light. Max slowed to a walk. This back street was quiet, no pedestrians about, no cars coming past. He took a turn and was glad to get onto the main road. He felt safer with the traffic streaming by and other people around him.

He walked rapidly back to King's Cross, his stomach churning with anxiety. Once or twice, he felt a prickle on the back of his neck and turned around, sure that someone was following him. But there was no one there.

He remained jittery all the way home, studying his fellow passengers on the Underground to see if they were taking an unusual interest in him, then looking over his shoulder continually as he half walked, half jogged the final few hundred yards to his house. Only when he was inside, the door locked and bolted behind him, did he relax a bit.

Consuela came out into the hall.

"Good game?" she asked

"Uh? Oh, the snooker. Yeah, good."

"Would you like something to drink?"

"No, thanks."

Consuela looked at him curiously. "You okay?"

"Yeah, I'm fine. I'll see you in the morning."

Max hung his jacket on the hook and went upstairs to bed.

4

MAX SLUMPED BACK ONTO HIS PILLOW AND stared up at his bedroom ceiling. The horrific vision of Luis Lopez-Vega's face was still imprinted vividly on his mind. That was all he could see. The bullet hole, the blood, those lifeless eyes . . .

He shuddered, wondering whether he'd done the right thing. Perhaps he should have gone down to the hotel reception and reported what he'd found, then waited for the police to arrive. He had nothing to hide, after all. He'd done nothing wrong. But it was too late to go back now. What good would it do, in any case? Lopez-Vega was dead. Max had no obvious information that might help the police find out who'd killed him. The more he thought about it, the more Max was sure that his initial reaction not to get involved had been correct.

What he had to try to do was put the body out of his mind. He took the piece of paper out of his pocket and concentrated on the numbers: 11138352. It was a simple sequence, but what did the numbers signify? What did they mean? And why had Luis Lopez-Vega concealed them on the underside of his wig? Max pondered these questions as he got ready for bed.

He found it hard to fall asleep. He lay awake for a long time, thinking about the numbers and Luis Lopez-Vega, wondering what the man knew about his dad. He worried about the hotel room too. Had he left any fingerprints behind? He'd wiped all the obvious surfaces, but maybe he'd missed somewhere important. He'd touched Lopez-Vega's clothes! Could the police get fingerprints from those? And was there anything else he might have forgotten, any other evidence to show that he'd been there? Had anyone seen him leaving? The very thought broke him out in a cold sweat, gave him palpitations.

In the morning, after a restless, troubled night, he was still worrying. He studied the piece of paper again over breakfast. Maybe the answer was something obvious. What if it was a phone number? Max punched the numbers into his cell but got only a mechanical, computer-generated voice telling him the number was not recognized.

What else could it be? A code of some sort? That was possible. Or what about a combination to a lock or a safe? That could be it too. If so, where was the safe?

"Max?"

Consuela touched him on the shoulder and he started violently. "You'd better get a move on, or you'll be late for school."

"What? Oh, yes."

Max bolted the rest of his toast and gulped down a mouthful of orange juice. He folded the piece of paper in two and was about to put it in his pocket when he realized there was no need for him to keep it. Eight numbers weren't hard to remember: 11138352—they were lodged in his brain already. *Keep them there,* he told himself, *where no one else can touch them, and destroy the written version.* Max tossed the piece of paper into the downstairs toilet and flushed it away.

The numbers continued to distract him all morning. Lessons passed him by in a haze, almost nothing registering on his brain. History, IT, English—they all seemed the same, just a tedious mixture of droning teachers and boring facts that were keeping Max away from the more important business of working out what the numbers meant.

At lunchtime, he didn't head for the cafeteria as usual, but went instead to the library, where he found a book on codes and ciphers. He leafed through the book, seeing if any of the more common kinds of code-breaking techniques could be applied to the eight numbers. He tried a simple system of matching the numbers to the letters of the alphabet—A = 1, B = 2, and so on—but just ended up with an incomprehensible jumble of letters. He tried other methods, reversing the alphabet, looking for patterns in the numbers, but nothing seemed to work. What he needed was some kind of code-breaking software that could crack the sequence, but neither the computers at school nor his home PC had such a program. Maybe it wasn't a code at all. Maybe he was simply wasting his time.

The afternoon went by in the same sort of soporific blur as the morning. Max was only vaguely aware of the lessons he had to sit through, impatiently waiting for the final bell, when he could escape and go somewhere quiet to think.

On the walk home from school, he was so wrapped up in himself that he didn't notice the three boys waiting for him until he was almost on top of them.

They'd chosen their spot carefully—the secluded path through a patch of woodland at the edge of the school playing fields that Max always took home. It was far enough away from both the school buildings and the surrounding houses to ensure that they weren't seen by anyone. It was the perfect place for an ambush.

"Well, look who we've got here," the biggest of the boys said. "If it isn't Max Cassidy. Or should that be 'The Great Maximilian'?"

Max stopped, gazing warily at the three boys—Harry Ross, the one who'd spoken, and his two companions, Dominic Mulgrew and Tom Sutcliffe. They were all two years older than him and had a reputation for violence and intimidation. Max knew he was in trouble.

"'The Great Maximilian'?" Ross repeated. "What kind of loser name is that?"

Max tried to walk around the three of them, but Ross stepped out to block his path.

"What's the hurry, Cassidy? You got somewhere to go? Like visiting your mum in jail? What's it like, eh? Having a mum who's a killer?"

Max resisted the urge to lash out at Ross, to punch him hard in his big fat face. He didn't want to get in a fight. He was outnumbered and, in any case, he couldn't afford to injure himself. A sprained wrist or a pulled muscle would mean having to cancel his next show.

"What do you want, Ross?" he asked.

"We want a little chat with you, don't we, guys?" Ross said, glancing at Mulgrew and Sutcliffe. "I asked you a question," he went on. "What's it like having a mum who's a murderer? A jailbird. Who else has she killed, apart from your dad? Shame she's locked up, or she could do us all a favor and knock you off, too."

Ross laughed, and Mulgrew and Sutcliffe joined in. Max looked around casually, seeing if he could get away, but the boys had positioned themselves around him, cutting off his escape. Max couldn't go forward, or to the sides, and he knew that if he attempted to retreat they'd jump on him immediately.

"You got any money on you?" Ross said.

"No, I haven't," replied Max.

"Yeah? A big star like you—you must be raking it in."

"I don't have any money on me," Max said. "Okay?"

He was used to the resentment and envy his show-business activities aroused in some of his fellow pupils and was always careful not to show off or brag, or flash money and possessions around at school. Not that he

53

had that much money. Since his dad's disappearance and his mum's imprisonment, his fees all went into a bank account to cover the mortgage and household bills and to pay for other expenses like food and clothes. When all that was taken care of, there was very little left for Max to spend on himself.

"Let's see what he's got, guys," Ross said.

Max backed away a couple of paces. "Look, I don't want any trouble," he said.

Ross smiled at him coldly. "But maybe we do."

Mulgrew and Sutcliffe grabbed hold of him, one on each side, and Ross hooked an arm around his neck, gripping him in a vicious headlock.

"If you're such a world-famous escapologist," taunted Ross, "get out of that."

He pulled Max's head down, still holding his neck tight. Max grunted with pain. It felt as if the bully was trying to screw his head off.

"You know what to do, guys," Ross said.

Max felt Mulgrew and Sutcliffe going through his pockets and backpack. He was powerless to stop them.

"A couple of quid," said Mulgrew eventually. "That's all."

"What about his bag?" Ross asked.

"Just a bunch of books."

"You hiding something, Cassidy?" Ross said, jerking at Max's head so a stab of pain lanced up his neck. "If you are, you're going to regret it."

Ross tightened his grip. Max knew he had to do something or he'd end up badly hurt. He didn't want to retaliate, but sometimes the only form of defense was attack. He brought his elbow back and hammered it hard into Ross's groin. Ross yelled an obscenity. He let go of Max and clutched at himself, his eyes watering. Before the others could react, Max was tearing away along the path.

The ground was rough and uneven, but Max was fast and agile. His feet skimmed over the stones and potholes, dodging tree roots and twigs. He burst out of the wood and sprinted down the hill toward some houses. Glancing back, he was dismayed to see the three thugs right on his tail. They were twenty or thirty yards back, but they were running hard, showing no sign of abandoning the chase.

Max slowed for the gate at the bottom of the hill, then whipped it open and raced through, heading along the passage that ran between two houses. The gang came after him, Ross describing in graphic detail what he was going to do to Max when he caught him.

At the end of the passage was the main road. As Max

skidded out onto the pavement, he saw a car parked by the curb, its rear door open.

A man leaned out through the door and waved urgently at Max. "Quick! In here."

Without thinking, Max jumped into the car and slammed the door shut. It was an impulse decision. He wanted only to get away from the thugs and he didn't care how. The car moved off just seconds before Ross and his mates hurtled out of the passage. Max twisted around to look through the back window. The three boys were bent over, hands on knees, gasping for breath. Ross looked up, staring hard at Max, his face twisted with anger and hate. The car kept going, speeding away up the road. Ross receded into the distance, getting smaller and smaller until finally he was lost from sight.

"Having a spot of trouble, Max?"

Max turned to look at the man next to him. Only then did he realize that he'd accepted a lift from a complete stranger without a second thought. He felt the hairs prickle on the back of his neck. The man was in his forties, short and plump, with red cheeks, a fleshy nose, and hair that was graying at the temples. He wore a smart black suit, a pale-pink shirt, and a gray silk tie, and he smelled of fresh aftershave.

"How do you know my name?" Max said. He was breathing heavily, his heart pounding.

"I know many things." The man clicked a switch on the armrest beside him and spoke to the driver through an intercom.

"Keep going around the block until I say stop, Mason."

The driver, separated from the back of the car by a thick, soundproof glass window, nodded and eased the car smoothly into a bend. It was a luxurious, top-of-the-line Mercedes with tinted windows, leather uphol-stery, a minibar, and a television built into the back of the front seat. Max couldn't hear the engine, it was so quiet, or feel the bumps in the road. It was as if the car were gliding along on a cushion of air.

"What's going on?" he asked. "Who are you?"

"My name is Rupert Penhall." The man smiled at Max, but there was no warmth in it. "I think we should have a little chat, don't you?"

A little chat? Max was struck by the similarity between Penhall's words and Harry Ross's. Neither time had the invitation sounded remotely enticing.

"A chat about what?" he demanded.

"Shall we start with dead bodies in hotel rooms?" Penhall said.

"I don't know what you're talking about," Max replied.

Penhall sighed. "I was hoping you weren't going to

be difficult, Max. You know what a CCTV camera is, of course?"

"Yes."

"Then let me tell you that on the foyer wall in the Rutland Hotel there's a CCTV camera. A CCTV camera that recorded you entering the building at just after eight yesterday evening."

Max didn't say anything.

"Shall we start again?" Penhall said.

"Are you a policeman?" asked Max.

Penhall gave a snort of laughter. "Good God, no. Do I look like a policeman? I sincerely hope not."

"What are you then?"

"Let's say I'm connected to the government."

Max stared at him contemptuously. He loathed the government. They were the people who'd stood by and done nothing while his mother was put on trial for a crime she obviously hadn't committed. The people who'd allowed her to be convicted and imprisoned, then left her languishing in a filthy Santo Domingo jail for eighteen months before belatedly negotiating her transfer to a prison in Britain.

"Do you have some ID?" Max said.

Penhall seemed offended by the question. "ID? People like me don't carry identification."

"So how do I know you're who you say you are?"

"You'll have to take it on trust."

Trust? Max almost laughed. The last person he was going to trust was this smooth, perfumed toad.

"What were you doing at the hotel?" Penhall demanded.

"What makes you think I was?" Max fired back. "CCTV pictures are always grainy. How do you know it was me?"

"Don't play games," snapped Penhall. "Let me spell it out for you. You cooperate with me now, or I turn you and the CCTV tape over to the police and you can explain to them why you left the scene of a murder."

Max was suddenly frightened. The mask had fallen away, and he saw that beneath all the smart trappings— the suit, the silk tie, the flashy car—Rupert Penhall was nothing but a thug. A grown-up, more sophisticated Harry Ross.

"Do you understand me?" Penhall said. "*Do* you?"

"Yes, I understand," Max said quietly.

"Well?"

"I went to see Luis Lopez-Vega."

"Why?"

"Because he asked me to."

"When did he ask you?"

"He came backstage after my show on Wednesday evening."

"You knew him?"

The questions were coming at Max like a salvo of gunfire.

"No, I'd never seen him before in my life."

"Did he say why he wanted to see you?"

"No."

Penhall looked at him suspiciously. "Are you sure?"

"Yes."

Penhall sniffed. "So this man you've never seen before asks you to go to his hotel and you go? I find that hard to believe."

"It's true," Max said.

"Describe to me what you found when you got there."

"His door was already open," Max said. "I went in and he was there on the floor. Dead."

"Did you touch his body?"

"No."

"Or anything in the room?"

"No."

"Nothing at all?"

"No."

Max wasn't going to tell him about the piece of paper with the numbers on it. He knew instinctively that he should be wary of Rupert Penhall.

"Why didn't you report it to the hotel manager?"

"I don't know," Max said. "I was scared. I'd never seen a dead body before. I suppose I just panicked, got out as quickly as I could. I didn't want anyone to think I'd done it."

"Why would anyone think you'd done it? A fourteen-year-old schoolboy?"

Max stared at him. "People get accused of things they haven't done," he said.

"You're referring to your mother, I presume?"

Max didn't answer. He looked out of the car window. They were driving past the local shopping center for the second time. Max wanted to get out—he felt like a prisoner in the back of the car—but he knew Penhall hadn't finished with him.

"Lopez-Vega mentioned your mother, didn't he?" Penhall said.

Max hesitated, wondering how much he should reveal. He decided he had more to gain by seeming to cooperate. Perhaps Penhall would let something slip that would be useful. "Yes, he mentioned her."

"What did he say?"

"That her trial was rigged."

"He was lying, Max. He knew nothing about your mother's trial."

"Didn't he?"

"Luis Lopez-Vega was a criminal and a con man. He was well known to the police in Santo Domingo. He had a conviction for drug dealing and spent the last two years in prison."

Was that what Lopez-Vega had meant when he said he'd been "away" for a while? It was possible. But he hadn't looked, or sounded, like a criminal, much less a drug dealer. Max had a hunch that Penhall wasn't telling him the whole truth.

"You'd do anything to clear your mother's name, wouldn't you, Max?" Penhall said.

"She's innocent," Max answered firmly.

"She was convicted by a court of law."

"A Santo Domingan court. Where the judge had been bribed."

"You don't know that. The evidence all pointed to your mother being the killer."

Max rounded on him furiously. "That's rubbish. She didn't do it."

"Your faith in her is touching," Penhall said sardonically.

"She didn't do it!" Max yelled at him. "And

I'm going to prove it."

The words just came out impulsively. But the moment he'd said them, Max knew that was exactly what he was going to do.

"And how exactly are you going to do that?"

"Why should you care? What have *you* ever done for her?"

"Her trial was a matter for the authorities in Santo Domingo. The British government can't interfere in the affairs of a foreign state."

"Can't it?" Max said bitterly.

"Let me give you a warning, Max," Penhall said, his voice low and menacing. "You're meddling in things you know nothing about. Continue meddling, and you may end up getting hurt. I'm sure that's something neither of us wants to happen. Do I make myself clear?"

He clicked on the intercom again and spoke to the driver. "Pull over here, Mason." The car glided to a stop by the curb. Penhall looked at Max. "You can get out now," he said, as if he were dismissing a servant.

Max pushed open the door, anger seething inside him. He glanced back at Penhall, who was lounging on the leather seat with a smug, self-satisfied smirk on his pudgy face.

Max slammed the door behind him and walked

away. The Mercedes pulled off and Max watched it purr past him, longing to pick up a stone and hurl it through the tinted back window at Penhall's head.

He was still furious when he got home. There was a note on the kitchen table from Consuela, telling him that she'd gone to the supermarket. Max was glad she wasn't there. He didn't feel like talking to anyone. He went upstairs to his room and lay down on the bed, thinking back over his conversation with Rupert Penhall. Conversation? It had been more like an interrogation.

A number of things didn't seem to make sense. A CCTV camera picked up a boy entering the Rutland Hotel. There were millions of teenage boys in London. How did Penhall identify him? Why, in any case, did Penhall have the tape? It was potentially important evidence in a murder inquiry. It might even show the killer entering or leaving the hotel, so why didn't the police have it rather than someone who was "connected to the government"? What did "connected to the government" mean, anyway?

There was also something suspicious about the way Penhall had just picked up Max. He had run out onto the street and the car had been there waiting for him. That was too much of a coincidence to believe. It was almost as if Penhall knew Max would be arriving at that point, at that time. Had someone been watching him, noting his route home from school?

And what about Ross and his mates? Why had they picked on him today? Why had they searched his clothes and his rucksack? *Don't be stupid,* Max said to himself. *You're getting paranoid.* But maybe he had good cause to be paranoid. He'd found a dead body in a hotel room; he'd been threatened by some kind of government official. What the hell was going on?

Max bit his thumbnail pensively, his eyes flickering about the room.

Something wasn't right. His CD rack had been moved. He could see the slight indentations in the carpet where it had originally been. And some books on the shelf were out of place too. Max inspected the rest of the room, checking the chest of drawers and his desk. He wasn't the tidiest of boys, and when he bent down he could see fresh smudge marks in the dust where someone—certainly not he—had smeared the surface of the desk with a hand or an arm.

His whole room had been searched. Had whoever had done it been looking for the numbers? Thank God he'd been clever enough to dispose of the piece of paper.

Max sat back down on his bed. Now he was really

scared. More scared than he'd ever been. Someone had broken into his house and searched his room. No, they hadn't broken in. That was what made it even more disturbing. They'd got in without leaving any trace of their entry. If Max wasn't so observant, he would never have known they'd been there. But who were "they"? The government? Someone else?

Max shivered, remembering Penhall's final few words to him. *You're meddling in things you know nothing about. Continue meddling, and you may end up getting hurt.*

5

THE NEXT DAY WAS SATURDAY, THE START OF the half-term holiday. Max had a show in the evening and spent most of the day at the London Cabaret Club, preparing himself and his equipment for the performance. He didn't have time to dwell too much on what had happened over the previous couple of days, but it was always there at the back of his mind, niggling away at him. Was his dad really alive? What did that mysterious sequence of numbers mean? Who was Rupert Penhall? Why had his bedroom been searched? Questions were going around and around inside his head without him finding any answers.

He was up early on Sunday morning. Max had mixed

feelings about Sundays. It should have been the one day of the week he looked forward to. His Saturday-evening show was out of the way; there was no school. He could see his friends, watch TV, do all those things that he never had time for during the rest of the week. But he didn't. On Sundays he went to visit his mother. He loved seeing her, but he hated seeing her in that place, seeing what prison had done to her.

This Sunday, however, he was eager to go. He had a lot of things to discuss with his mum. Consuela drove him there, northeast through the suburbs of London and then on into Suffolk. Levington Prison was a modern establishment, built only a few years earlier. It was a clean, relatively comfortable place—certainly compared to the old Victorian prisons in London where three or four inmates were shut up in one cell for twenty-three hours a day—but it was still a prison. It had a high mesh perimeter fence topped with razor wire and, inside that, a thirteen-foot-high concrete wall that was floodlit at night and monitored continuously by CCTV cameras.

The cells were all in a four-story central block. Max had never been in one, but he knew from his mother that they each contained a bed, a desk, a toilet, and a washbasin. She'd told him once that her small cell window looked out over the rolling countryside toward the sea. She'd said it to try to cheer him up, to try and make him think that prison wasn't all bad. But to Max it seemed just another particularly cruel touch. To see the fields and woods around the prison and yet be aware all the time that she couldn't walk in any of them, to see the ocean on the distant horizon and know that she couldn't paddle in it or lie on the beach in the sun—that must be unbearable.

Consuela parked in the fenced lot outside the prison wall. Max left her in the car and went in alone.

Max was used to the security measures by now, but they still felt intrusive and humiliating. All bags were searched, and the contents of pockets had to be emptied into a plastic tray. You then had to walk through a metal detector and take off your shoes to be inspected before a uniformed guard gave you a pat-down search, looking for concealed weapons or other forbidden items.

After that, you were escorted through a locked steel door and along a windowless corridor to the visiting area. The visiting area was big, about the size of a school hall, and lined with rows of plain wooden tables that each had two plastic chairs drawn up next to them.

Max sat down at one of the tables and waited.

Around him, other visitors were also waiting. There was a wide range of people—middle-aged women, pensioners, young men, some alone, some accompanied by children. Max knew many of the regulars. A few nodded at him in greeting.

Five minutes later, a door at the far end of the hall opened and a group of prisoners was escorted in by a guard, Helen Cassidy among them. She smiled with pleasure as she saw Max and walked quickly across the room to meet him. Max stood up and they hugged—a long, tight hug that he never wanted to end. His mother broke away. There were tears in her eyes and Max felt his own eyes begin to prickle. He sat down again and blinked hard to stop himself from crying.

"How are you, Max?" his mother asked, sitting opposite him.

"I'm okay. You?"

"I'm fine."

She didn't look fine. Prison was aging her. When she'd first come back to England, she'd looked drawn and haggard, her health eroded by the poor conditions she'd endured in the Santo Domingan prison. She had started to look better during her time at Levington, but she was still pale and thin. Her face was lined, her hair lank and unkempt. She had once taken pride in her appearance, but prison had destroyed it.

She smiled at him again. She always tried to be cheerful when he came to visit. Max knew it was just an act. Underneath, she was suffering badly.

"How's Consuela?" Helen asked.

"She's okay."

"And your shows this week? How did they go? Did you do any new tricks?"

"They went well," Max said.

He told her about his shows, though he didn't mention the water-tank escape going wrong on Wednesday. She had enough on her plate without worrying about him. Then they talked briefly about what he'd done at school, Max doing his best to cheer his mum up.

"What've you got on this week?" she asked.

"It's half-term."

She sat back, her face falling. "Oh, yes, of course. I'd forgotten."

Max could see the hurt in his mother's eyes. School holidays were particularly difficult for her. In the past they'd have done things as a family at half-term—gone away for a few days, visited the swimming pool, or gone to the cinema. Knowing Max would be off from school while she was locked up in her cell made her situation all the more distressing.

"What're you going to do?" Helen asked. "Have you and Consuela got anything planned?"

"No, haven't really thought about it."

Max disliked this kind of small talk. It seemed so unimportant, so irrelevant next to all the unspoken things that were boiling up inside both of them. These visits were torture for him, and for Helen, too. Seeing each other for half an hour a week in a room full of other people, the prison guards always hovering in the background—it was agony. Max couldn't bear to think of his mother shut away in this terrible place for the next eighteen years. His mother, all alone in a tiny cell, slowly withering away. She was putting on a brave face, but prison wasn't just aging her. It was killing her.

Max glanced at the clock on the visiting-room wall. He couldn't hold it in any longer. "Mum, I need to talk to you," he said. "About a man who came to see me after the show on Wednesday. His name was Luis Lopez-Vega. Does that name mean anything to you?"

"I don't think so," she replied.

"He came from Santo Domingo."

Helen Cassidy frowned. "From Santo Domingo?"

"He said he saw Dad's act there. He said he knew that you were innocent, that the judge in your trial had been bribed."

"I've never heard of him. Did he say he'd met us in Santo Domingo?"

"No. We didn't have time to talk much."

"What did he look like?"

"Tall and thin with dark skin and black hair. A wig. Underneath he was completely bald. Oh, and he had two missing fingers on his left hand."

Max's mother stared at him pensively, her brow furrowing again. "Two missing fingers?"

"That's right. You *do* know him, don't you?"

"There *was* a man," Helen said. "In the hotel bar the day your father disappeared. He and Alex spoke briefly. I remember noticing his hand and wondering what had happened to it."

"Do you know what he and Dad spoke about?" Max asked.

"I didn't hear. I was sitting at a table. Your dad went to the bar to order us some drinks. I wasn't really paying much attention. When I looked round, I saw them talking together. The man was gesturing with his hand—that's why I saw he'd lost two fingers—but I was too far away to hear what they were saying."

"You've never mentioned him before."

"Why should I? We spoke to dozens of people at the hotel during our stay. People were always coming up to your dad, talking to him about his act. It was a bit annoying, really, but he was always polite. He was doing the show in the hotel theater, as you know, so these people were his audience. He had to be friendly to them."

"Did you see the man again?" Max asked.

"Not that I recall."

"Did Dad see him again?"

"If he did, he never said anything to me. What is this, Max?"

Max glanced at the clock again. He didn't have much time. "Mum, I don't want to upset you. I know you've told me this many times before, but I want you to describe for me again exactly what happened in Santo Domingo."

"Oh, Max, what's the use?" Helen sighed. "It won't make any difference. It won't change anything."

"You'd forgotten about the man with the missing fingers," Max said. "Maybe there's something else you've forgotten. Something that might be significant."

"Everything significant has already come out, Max, and it hasn't made a difference, I'm still here," Helen said. "The man at the bar was irrelevant."

"Please, Mum. I know it's hard for you, but tell me again."

She looked away across the hall, composing herself. Then she began to speak, her voice low and tremulous. She'd repeated this story so many times—to the Santo Domingo police, to her lawyer, to the judge at her trial—that the words came out automatically, as if she were an actress reciting lines from a play.

Alex Cassidy had been invited to Santo Domingo to do two shows at a tourist resort named Playa d'Oro, just outside the capital, Rio Verde. Helen and Consuela had gone with him, Consuela to assist with the shows, Helen to have a holiday while Max was away on his school trip.

"We arrived on the Monday evening," Helen said. "Alex had a show on Tuesday evening and another on Wednesday, in the hotel's theater. Playa d'Oro was a strange place. I didn't like it much, nor did your father. It had been specially built as a resort for wealthy westerners, but it was like a prison." She smiled grimly. "It had a high fence all around it and a main gate with a checkpoint manned by armed guards to keep out the locals. The only Santo Domingans allowed into Playa d'Oro were employees—cooks, waiters, and cleaners. Everybody else was kept out.

"It felt wrong. On one side of the fence, you had the local people, mostly very poor, living in shanty-towns without running water or drains. And on the other side, you had this incredibly luxurious holiday resort. And it was *really* luxurious. Huge suites that cost thousands of dollars a night, seven or eight different restaurants serving wonderful food, four swimming pools, a golf course, a casino, riding stables . . . It had everything you could wish for.

"The theater was vast. It must have held two thousand people easily. And every night there was a show. The management flew in acts from all around the world—dancing troupes, magicians, orchestras, famous pop stars. And your father."

"You'd never been there before, had you?" Max said.

"No, it was our first time. I wasn't sure about going there, but your dad was keen to explore a new place, see new things."

"So Dad did his shows in the evening. But what did you do during the day?"

"Went to the beach, swam, saw the sights. I went riding one afternoon and your father went fishing."

"Yes, I remember you telling me that," Max said. "It's always seemed odd. Dad wasn't interested in fishing."

"I know. I think he just wanted to get away from the resort—it was so exclusive, so unreal, like a theme park. He went into Rio Verde. There was a harbor there where you could charter a boat. He went out with a local skipper, Fernando Gonzales. Your father said he caught a six-foot marlin and threw it back, but I didn't believe him."

Helen smiled briefly—a sad smile—as she remembered that moment. "You know how Dad liked to tell stories."

"Did you meet this Fernando Gonzales?" Max asked.

Helen shook her head. "I know the police interviewed him. Apparently they interviewed almost everyone we'd met while we were in Santo Domingo. But he had nothing to do with your father's disappearance. He was just a poor local fisherman trying to supplement his income by taking western tourists out in his boat."

"And the night Dad disappeared?" prompted Max.

"It was the Thursday evening," Helen said. "We went back to our room. There were these straw-roofed bungalows down by the beach, and the hotel management had given us one for our stay. I was packing our cases—we had an early flight home the next morning—and your father left me and went over to the theater to check all his equipment was correctly packaged for the journey back to England. Consuela was waiting for him there but, as you know, he never showed up."

Helen had finished her packing and was getting ready for bed when Consuela came to the bungalow looking for Alex. Neither woman was unduly concerned that he hadn't arrived at the theater—not at that point, anyway. They assumed he must have been sidetracked. Perhaps he was having a drink in the bar, or maybe he'd gone for a last walk along the beach. It was only when it got past midnight and Alex still hadn't returned that Helen and Consuela raised the alarm. The hotel manager dispatched a team of security guards to search the resort, but they found no sign of Alex anywhere. It was then that the local police were called in.

This second, more thorough search of the resort was no more successful than the first. Max's father seemed to have vanished into thin air. The guards at the main gate—which was the only way in and out of Playa d'Oro—were certain that he hadn't come past. The perimeter fence was too high to climb, and an inspection confirmed that no holes had been cut through the wire. That left only the sea as a possible exit.

At dawn the next morning, the shoreline was closely examined by the police. Alex's jacket and wallet were found by some rocks near the Cassidys' bungalow, then traces of blood and, in a cleft in the rocks, a blood-stained knife. More blood was then discovered in a small rowing boat pulled up on the beach—one of the boats provided for the use of hotel guests. Forensic tests later showed that the blood type matched Alex's and that fingerprints on both the knife and the rowing boat were Helen's. Helen was arrested, charged with the murder of her husband, and convicted by a Santo Domingan court, despite the fact that Alex's body had never been found.

"What more can I say?" Helen said to Max. "You know the details as well as I do. The prosecutor said I stabbed your dad, put his body in the boat, and rowed out to sea, where I dumped him overboard. The judge had already decided I was guilty. My fingerprints were on the knife, weren't they? Well, of course they were. The knife had been taken from our bungalow. I don't know when. We had a small kitchenette where we could make drinks or light snacks. I'd used the knife several times to cut up fruit.

"And my fingerprints on the boat? I'd touched it earlier that same evening. Your dad and I had gone down at dusk to watch the sunset, and we'd sat on the edge of the boat together. There were witnesses who'd seen us there, but that didn't make any difference. The judge didn't want to hear any evidence that might contradict the prosecution's case. As if I'd kill your father. As if I'd do anything like that. . . ." Helen's voice cracked with emotion. She lifted a finger and brushed away a tear from her eye.

Max took his mother's hand in his own and squeezed it. "I didn't mean to upset you, Mum. We both know you didn't do it. I just want to examine the facts again, see if there's anything we've missed."

"I've been examining them inside my head for the past two years," Helen said. "I've missed nothing. But I'm no nearer to working out what happened to your father, and no nearer to proving that I didn't kill him."

"There must be something," Max said. "Why would anyone want to murder Dad? If that's what really happened."

Helen gazed at her son gently. "Oh, Max. You're not still hoping he's alive, are you?"

"Luis Lopez-Vega said he was."

Helen stared at him, her mouth gaping. "He said your dad was alive?"

"Yes."

"Oh, Max." Helen took hold of his other hand and gripped it tight. "Don't get your hopes up. If he is alive, where has he been for the past two years? Why hasn't he come home, gotten me out of prison?"

"I don't know, Mum. I just know I miss him. I miss him so much."

"We both do, Max. But you have to accept he's gone."

Helen held his eyes for a long time, until Max could bear it no longer and had to look away.

"Maybe Luis Lopez-Vega was telling the truth," he said.

"What exactly did he say?"

Max glanced around the room. There was no prison officer nearby, but he lowered his voice anyway, telling his mother about seeing Lopez-Vega at the theater and then his visit to the Rutland Hotel.

Her eyes opened wide in horror. *"Dead!"* she exclaimed. "Oh, my God! Max, I don't want you getting mixed up in this. It's not safe."

"I'm mixed up in it already," Max said. "It's too late. The room at the hotel had been searched, but I found something under Lopez-Vega's wig—a piece of paper with eight numbers on it. One-one-one-three-eight-three-five-two. Do they mean anything to you?"

"Give them to me again."

Max repeated the numbers. "I think they might be a code, or a combination," he said.

Helen thought for a while, then shook her head. "I

don't know what they are."

"Keep thinking about them. Whatever they are, they're important. If anything comes to you, let me know next week."

A guard walked past their table and murmured, "Two minutes."

"One last thing," Max said quickly. "Have you ever come across a man named Rupert Penhall? Small, fat, red-faced, says he's connected to the government?"

"No, I don't think so. Look, Max, I don't know what you're doing, but I want you to stop. I'm worried about you."

"I'm okay."

"You found a dead body. That's not okay."

Max leaned forward over the table, his eyes alight with determination. "We have to get you out of here, Mum. We have to clear your name."

Helen gazed back at him. She could see the fire in Max's face, but there was nothing in hers save a weary resignation. "What's the use, Max?" she said dejectedly. "They're never going to reopen my case. We have to face up to reality. I'm going to be in here for the next eighteen years."

"No, no you're not," Max said forcefully. "I'm going to get you out. I promise."

"You're such a good boy, Max. But it's not going to happen."

"*It is*," Max insisted, so violently that the other prisoners and their visitors looked around at him.

The guard was coming across the hall now to take Helen back to her cell.

"It is," Max said again more quietly.

They stood up.

"Thanks for coming. I'll see you next week," Helen said. "Look after yourself. And I mean it about not getting mixed up in anything. You're all I've got, Max. Take care. I love you."

They hugged once more. Max watched his mother being led away, fighting back the tears. Over the last two years he'd come to terms with his father's disappearance. But each time he left his mother behind in prison, he felt as if he were losing her again.

It was all becoming too much for him. He wanted the pain to end. He wanted to find out what had really happened to his father. He wanted to get his mother out of prison.

And he would.

6

CONSUELA DIDN'T TALK TO MAX MUCH ON the drive back to London. She could see he was absorbed in his own thoughts. He was often like this after visiting Levington. Seeing his mother made him pensive, introverted. He'd be quiet and withdrawn for a few hours, but Consuela knew he would snap out of it if she gave him some time to himself. It was understandable. Who wouldn't get depressed by visiting his mother in prison? Particularly a mother who shouldn't have been there in the first place.

When they got home, Max went upstairs to his bedroom and sat at his desk, gazing out of the window at the garden without really seeing anything. All his energy, his thoughts, were focused on the events of the past few days and all the unanswered questions troubling him.

Today, after everything that had happened, Max didn't feel down—he felt angry. His body was tense and he clenched and unclenched his fists. His mother's situation was so wrong, so unjust, but what could he do? Where should he direct his fury? At the Santo Domingan police? The Santo Domingan courts? The British government? Max was angry with them all. But what use was anger? Anger wouldn't get his mother out of prison. It wouldn't clear her name. It wouldn't help him find out whether his father was still alive. Only action could do that.

He'd waited long enough. At the beginning, he'd thought that somehow everything would sort itself out. That the Santo Domingans would realize they'd made a mistake and release his mother. Or that the British government would see she'd been wrongfully imprisoned and do something about it. But nothing had happened.

His mother had a lawyer in Santo Domingo who was supposed to be representing her, trying to get her case reopened, but he was getting nowhere. The British government was equally useless. Despite several appeals from his mother, they had made no attempt to put pressure on the Santo Domingans to look at her conviction again.

Max knew now that he'd been naïve. He'd spent too long relying on others. If anything was going to happen, he was going to have to do it himself.

But how?

Where did he begin?

He reflected for a moment, then turned on his computer. He'd done some research on Santo Domingo when his mother had first been imprisoned there, but he'd forgotten a lot of it. He needed to refresh his memory, remind himself how the country worked, how its political and legal systems operated.

He clicked on a few websites and read through them. Santo Domingo was a tiny country in Central America, so small that most people had never heard of it. Fifty miles long and about half that in width, it was dwarfed by the nearby, much larger states of Honduras, Nicaragua, and Costa Rica. Santo Domingo seemed to have kept its independence only because there was nothing much there that anyone wanted. It had no oil, no natural gas, no minerals, no timber, just swamps and a lot of mosquitoes. The Spanish had conquered it in the sixteenth century, stripping it of its gold and other valuables and wiping out most of the native population in the process. It had then remained a Spanish colony until the mid-nineteenth century, when it was granted independence and the freedom to manage its own affairs.

For more than a hundred years thereafter the country was run by a succession of military dictators, each as brutal and incompetent as the last, until, in the 1970s, a nationwide uprising removed the last of the generals and brought democracy and fair elections to Santo Domingo. The leader of the Partido Democrático Popular—the Democratic Popular Party or PDP—was a teacher named Juan Cruz, who became the president and spent two years reforming the country. He established a national health service, provided free education for all children, and took land away from the rich and gave it to peasant farmers. This made the generals, who also happened to be wealthy landowners themselves, decide that democracy wasn't such a good idea. They staged a military coup, assassinated Juan Cruz, and seized back control.

Then followed a period of savage repression. The PDP was banned, political opponents of the ruling regime were rounded up and imprisoned or shot, and the country returned to the squalor and poverty that it had endured under every previous military government.

Once the generals were firmly back in power, they restored the land to the rich landowners and took their revenge on the peasants. A large area of coastal territory near the capital that had belonged to small independent farmers was confiscated and sold to an international consortium of property developers, who proved just as greedy as the Spanish conquistadors.

Santo Domingo didn't have much going for it in terms of resources, but it did have two things that rich western tourists could appreciate—sun and sand. So the developers built the resort of Playa d'Oro, which meant "golden beach," and turned Santo Domingo into a haven for the wealthy. Some came there simply for holidays, but many more came to live in the resort, for Santo Domingo's other major advantage was very low taxes for the superrich. In fact, *no* taxes for the super-rich, if they knew who to bribe—and that wasn't very hard, as *everyone* in the government was on the take.

This last bit of information wasn't on any official Santo Domingo website but on one set up by the PDP. Though the party was still banned, it was apparently active underground. It was from this source that Max gleaned several other interesting pieces of information. The average annual salary of a Santo Domingan worker at Playa d'Oro was the equivalent of two hundred

U.S. dollars. The average room price per night for a guest at Playa d'Oro was five hundred dollars, and the "President's Suite" cost ten thousand dollars a night. The annual profit of the corporation that owned Playa d'Oro—in which the generals were leading shareholders—was two hundred million dollars.

The free health and education services that Juan Cruz had established had been abolished by the military regime, with the result that three children in ten died before they reached the age of five, and 50 percent of those under fifteen couldn't read or write. But there were more millionaires per square mile than anywhere else on earth.

There were no elections, the local police were thugs who tortured prisoners, and the judges—all appointed by the generals—openly demanded bribes to "fix" the cases that appeared before them.

Max read all this with a mounting sense of dismay. If it was true—and it had a horribly plausible ring to it—then getting justice for his mother in Santo Domingo was not going to be easy, or cheap. In fact, it looked to him as if there was no such thing as justice in the country. It was simply a question of who could pay the most.

He gazed out of the window again, thinking about where he went from here. He knew a bit more about

Santo Domingo now, and if he'd learned one thing it was this: He was never going to be able to help his mother from here in London. If he was going to secure her release, he had to go to Santo Domingo.

At dinner that evening, Max set to work on Consuela. He could do nothing without her help.

"I'm sorry I was a bit off with you today," he said.

"That's okay, I understand," she replied.

She smiled at him affectionately. Max smiled back, thinking how important she was to him. He had no memories at all of the time before she'd become his father's assistant as a girl of eighteen. She was a former gymnast and dancer who had been working in a traveling Spanish circus when Alexander Cassidy spotted her and asked her to come and work for him.

Now in her early thirties, she was a very attractive woman with the slender, lithe build of a dancer and flamboyant Mediterranean good looks. She received dozens of fan letters every week, some of them proposing marriage, and there was always a crowd of attentive well-wishers hanging around the stage door of the London Cabaret Club on show nights—and the men weren't there to see Max.

She had had several boyfriends over the years, but

none recently—not since Max's mother had been imprisoned. She'd put her personal life on hold, waiting for Max to grow up and become fully independent before she resumed her own life. She'd never said as much, but Max knew that was what she was doing.

"I've been thinking," Max said. He took a mouthful of the seafood paella Consuela had made. "This is really good, by the way."

"What about?" she asked.

"My mum. I'm worried about her. She's not coping well with prison. I can see her health is getting worse."

"That shouldn't be happening," Consuela said. "We can ring the prison, tell them to get a doctor for her."

"It's not a doctor she needs," Max said. "It's her freedom. She puts on a show for me every Sunday, but I can tell she's really depressed. I can see it in her face. She's not going to improve until she gets out, and that could be a long time."

"We're doing all we can for her."

"Are we?"

"You think we could be doing more?"

"I think we're relying too much on other people," Max said. "These lawyers who are supposed to be acting for her—Malcolm Fielding here in London and the one in Santo Domingo . . . what's his name? Estevez?"

"Yes, Alfonso Estevez."

"What are they actually *doing*? Apart from charging us a lot of money."

"The law is expensive," Consuela said. "It takes time to make things happen."

"It's taking too long," Max insisted. "I don't think they're trying. The months are ticking by, the *years* are ticking by, and what have they achieved? The case hasn't even gone to appeal in Santo Domingo yet, the Foreign Office here is refusing to intervene, and Mum's still stuck in prison. By the time anything happens— and we don't know it will—it's going to be too late for Mum, and me. I'm not going to wait around any longer. I want to do something. Now."

"Do what?"

"Go to Santo Domingo and speed things up."

Consuela looked at him, frowning slightly. "It's not that easy, Max," she said gently. "I've been to Santo Domingo. It's not the kind of place where anything happens quickly."

"But we stand a better chance of doing something there than we do here," Max said. "We can talk to Estevez face-to-face instead of by email and letter. We can look for new evidence to prove that Mum is innocent."

"New evidence? What makes you think there might be new evidence?"

Max ate some more paella. It was time to tell Consuela about Luis Lopez-Vega.

"Promise you won't be angry with me," he said.

"About what?"

"You remember on Wednesday night, after the show, there was a man in my dressing room?"

"Yes, I remember."

"He came from Santo Domingo. He told me not to tell anyone about his visit. That's why I haven't mentioned him before."

"From Santo Domingo?"

"His name was Luis Lopez-Vega. Mum didn't recognize the name when I told her this morning, but she recognized his description. He had two missing fingers on his left hand. She said my dad spoke to him in the bar at Playa d'Oro."

"I don't know the name either," Consuela said. She paused. "At least, I think I don't. Just a moment. *Luis Lopez-Vega?* That rings a bell."

She got up from the table and came back with the Sunday newspaper they'd picked up that morning on their way to Suffolk. She leafed through the pages for a while. "I knew I'd seen it somewhere. Here." She folded the newspaper and showed Max.

At the bottom of the page was a short article head-lined DRUGS LINK TO BODY IN HOTEL ROOM. Max read the article.

> *Police investigating the murder of a Central American man in a London hotel have revealed that the victim may have been an international drug dealer.*
>
> *Luis Lopez-Vega was found dead on Thursday evening in his room at the Rutland Hotel, near King's Cross. He had been shot through the head and robbed.*
>
> *A police spokesman said that Lopez-Vega had served time in jail in Santo Domingo for drug-related offenses and may have been in London to meet European drug dealers. The spokesman added that they were following up a number of leads but did not yet know why Lopez-Vega had been killed.*

Max felt relieved as he finished the story. There was no mention of a teenage boy having been seen arriving at or leaving the hotel. For the time being, at least, he was safe.

"Is that the man who came to your dressing room?" Consuela asked. "A drug dealer?" Her voice was rising, her cheeks starting to flush.

Max recognized the familiar signs of anger and tried to placate her. "He wasn't a drug dealer." Rupert Penhall had told him that, but he still didn't believe it.

"And how do you know that?"

"I could tell."

"Oh, you could *tell*, could you?" Consuela said. "How? There are a lot of drugs in Santo Domingo, you know. They bring cocaine up from Colombia and then ship it out from there to Europe and America."

"The police are wrong, or someone's lying to them. Lopez-Vega wasn't a drug dealer."

"How can you be sure?"

"A gut feeling. I met him, talked to him. He was an honest man, not a criminal. Now please, stop getting cross with me. I'm sorry I didn't tell you this earlier."

"But what has this man got to do with your mother?" Consuela asked.

Max described his encounter with Lopez-Vega, then told Consuela about his visit to the Rutland Hotel. He got the same horrified reaction as he'd had from his mother.

"Dear God, Max, what are you playing at? This is terrible. You must go to the police at once."

"I can't. I can't get involved," Max said. "It's too late; I'd get into big trouble. Besides, I don't know anything that would help them." He was uncomfortable. Consuela didn't get angry very often, but when she did, you knew about it. "I panicked. The dead body frightened me," he told her. "You have to understand. He said that Dad was alive, that Mum was innocent. That's why I went there. I had to find out what he knew. Those numbers under his wig—one-one-one-three-eight-three-five-two—have you any idea what they might be?"

"No, no idea at all. This man was murdered, Max. Someone shot him. Have you thought about that? You don't want to take this any further. I have very bad memories of Santo Domingo. It's a nasty, dangerous country. It's not suitable for children."

"I'm not a child," Max said.

"No, not a child. But not a grown-up, either."

"You'll be with me."

"No, Max."

"*Please*, Consuela," Max begged. "I can't do it without you. I can't fly alone, book a hotel, any of those things."

Consuela shook her head. "It's not a good idea. I'm responsible for you, Max. It's better to leave these matters to the lawyers."

"But that's my *point*," Max said in exasperation. "We *have* been leaving matters to the lawyers, and they've done nothing."

"You don't know that there's any new evidence to find in Santo Domingo."

"And we *won't* know if we don't look."

He put down his knife and fork and gazed intently at Consuela. "Look, this is the ideal time to go. It's half-term. We have no shows this week. We could just fly out for a few days, talk to Mum's lawyer and the police. If we find nothing, okay, we just come home. But if we do find something, then the trip will have been worth it. What do we have to lose?"

It was a good argument, but Max could see that Consuela was going to need more persuading. "My dad could be alive," he said.

"Or this Lopez-Vega could've been lying."

"He came all the way to England from Santo Domingo to lie to me? Why would he do that? He wasn't a rich man. And he wasn't well. A poor, sick man traveled five thousand miles to tell me a lie about my dad? Why?"

Consuela said nothing. Max could sense that she was wavering. "We can't afford to pass up this opportunity.

If we go to Santo Domingo, find out more about Lopez-Vega, maybe we can discover what he knew about Dad. And maybe we can help Mum. She's rotting in prison. You know she is. If we don't do something now, she's only going to get worse. We have to go to Santo Domingo, Consuela. We have to do it for *her*."

Consuela studied his face—the glow in his eyes, the fierce determination in the set of his jaw. She knew that he'd never forgive her if she refused him.

"Please, Consuela," Max said. "Trust me on this one. Nothing is more important to me. Nothing." He took hold of her hands and gazed imploringly into her eyes. "Please."

Consuela looked away. Her anger had gone now. After a few moments, she finally spoke. "How do we buy the tickets?"

7

THERE WERE NO DIRECT FLIGHTS FROM Britain to Santo Domingo, so they flew British Airways from Heathrow to Miami and then changed to a Santo Domingan Airlines flight for the remainder of their journey. On the first leg to Miami, the plane was a standard 747 jumbo jet full of families traveling economy class for holidays in Florida. The second leg was completely different. This plane—a Boeing 767—had been specially modified so that most of it was first or business class. The economy section, where Max and Consuela were seated, took up only a few rows at the rear of the plane.

Max could smell the money around them even

before they boarded the flight. The passengers were mostly couples or single businessmen. There were very few families and no young children at all. The men all had millionaires' suntans and expensive Rolex watches. The women were younger than their partners and all looked the same to Max—blond, heavily made up, and dripping with jewelry.

Max and Consuela were in a row of three seats, Max by the window, Consuela in the middle. The aisle seat was occupied by a youngish, ginger-haired man in a suit and tie who introduced himself as Derek Pratchett, a sales executive from London who was traveling to Santo Domingo on business.

"It's my first time, but I hear it's a fabulous place," he said. "Have you been before?" He leaned forward to address the question to Max.

"No," Max said.

"So what are you going there for?"

"Nothing much," Max replied.

"'Nothing much'? It's an awful long way to go for *nothing much*. Are you on holiday?"

"Sort of."

"What's your name?"

"Max."

"Max, eh? I have a cousin called Max—sells

stationery in Northampton. Is that short for Maxwell, or Maximilian?"

"It's just Max."

"My cousin is Maxwell, though no one calls him that. Well, except his mother. And is this *your* mother?" Pratchett looked inquiringly at Consuela, but the question was directed at Max.

"No, we're just together," Max told him.

"Is that right? And your parents, where are they?"

"They're not here," Max snapped, wishing this annoying little man would shut up.

"Where are you staying in Santo Domingo?" Pratchett asked.

"I can't remember."

"Not at Playa d'Oro? That's where everyone else is going. I've read about that place. It's supposed to be the world's most luxurious holiday resort. Did you know that? There's a casino there where you can win a million dollars on a slot machine. Imagine that, eh? A million dollars. What would you do, Max—you did say your name was Max, didn't you?—what would you do with a million dollars? I can tell you what I'd do. . . ."

Max switched off and looked out of the window as Pratchett described in minute detail exactly what he would do with a million dollars. It was an hour-long flight to Santo Domingo, but it was going to feel like ten with this bloke rabbiting on next to them. Consuela, wisely, had taken out a book from her hand luggage and was deeply engrossed in it—or pretending to be.

Max gazed out at the hazy sky. He was thinking ahead to Santo Domingo, planning what they were going to do when they got there. He was excited, but apprehensive. He was going to the place where his dad had disappeared, where his mum had been convicted of murder. That was a daunting prospect.

On arrival at the Santo Domingo airport, they had to stand in line to get through Immigration Control. Most passengers were waved past with barely a glance at their passports, but Max and Consuela were stopped and questioned. The immigration officer—a small, unshaven man in a grubby white shirt—examined their passports at length, occasionally glancing up to compare their photographs with their faces. Max watched him nervously. Why were they being singled out for special attention? Suddenly, Penhall's sinister warning came back to him. Was someone on the lookout for them? Had the Santo Domingan authorities been tipped off about their arrival? Max felt sick with anxiety.

"You are here for how long?" the immigration officer said in accented English.

"Until the end of the week," Consuela replied in Spanish.

"Purpose of visit?" The immigration officer lapsed gratefully back into his own language.

"Holiday."

"Nothing else?"

"No, just holiday. Why else do people come to Santo Domingo?"

The immigration officer stamped their passports and handed them back. "Enjoy your stay."

There was a bus waiting outside the arrivals terminal to take them into the capital. Derek Pratchett was sitting near the front of the bus. He gestured at a couple of empty seats across the aisle from him, but Max pretended not to see him and found two seats farther back instead.

It was a forty-minute journey along the coast to Rio Verde, the road twisting and turning past tiny coves in which huge waves broke over outcrops of rock, filling the air with fine sea spray. There were farms on the landward side of the carriageway, small, dusty fields of sugarcane and beans dotted with tumbledown farmhouses and toiling peasants in straw hats. Beyond the farms, the hills ascended steeply into the sky, their flanks carpeted in thick, green rainforest.

As they neared the capital, the farms and rainforest gave way to sprawling shantytowns—huts built from scraps of timber and rusty metal panels, their roofs little more than plastic sheets flapping in the wind. Max could see the center of Rio Verde in the distance. There were old colonial mansions lining the hillside above the harbor, yachts moored in the shallows near the mouth of the river that gave the capital its name.

A couple of miles offshore, an island rose up out of the sea, its sheer cliffs topped by a massive stone fortress that had towers and battlements, just like an English castle.

"What's that?" Max asked Consuela, pointing out of the bus window at the island.

"It's called the Isla de Sombra—Shadow Island," Consuela replied.

"It looks interesting. Can people visit it?"

"No, it's privately owned. By a rich businessman, I think, or maybe a multinational corporation. We were told about it when we were here before. It used to be a pirate stronghold back in the sixteenth century; then it was a Spanish fort and, for a time, an English one. More recently, it was used as a prison, I believe."

There was a better view of the island from the main square of Rio Verde, where the bus dropped off Max and Consuela and a few of the other passengers. Most people stayed on board. They were traveling to Playa d'Oro, which was fifteen minutes farther on, in the wide bay to the north of the capital.

Max looked out to sea. Shadow Island loomed up on the horizon, its high walls catching the rays of the setting sun, the sea around it streaked with silvery light. It was a picturesque sight, but something about the fortress unsettled Max.

"Where's your hotel?" Derek Pratchett asked, suddenly popping up behind them.

"I'm not sure," Max said vaguely.

"I've got a map here. Perhaps I can help you find it."

"It's okay, we can manage," replied Max.

"What's its name?"

"We'll be okay. Thanks—it was nice meeting you."

"Maybe we'll see each other again. Rio Verde's only a small place," Pratchett said.

God, I hope not, Max thought. "Yes, maybe," he said. "See you."

They picked up their bags, and Consuela asked a passerby for directions to the hotel they'd booked over the internet. Most western visitors to Santo Domingo went to Playa d'Oro, but that was too expensive for Max and Consuela. Besides, Consuela didn't want to go back to the resort. Not after what had happened last time she was there.

The Hotel San Rafael was in the Old Town, up a steep flight of steps on the hillside overlooking the river. It was a dilapidated place that had seen better days, but it was cheap and clean. Max and Consuela didn't need anything more luxurious.

They were tired and jet-lagged after the long journey, so they ate dinner in the hotel restaurant and then went up to their rooms. Max washed and brushed his teeth at the chipped washbasin, then wandered over to the window. The wooden shutters were partially closed. Max pushed them back and leaned on the windowsill, looking out over the dark city. The air was warm and humid. He could smell the aromas of onions and spices wafting up from a restaurant farther down the hill and, beneath that, the salty tang of the ocean gusting in on the breeze. Both sides of the river were speckled with pinpricks of light, lamps shining through the windows of houses and flickering on boats in the harbor.

Max turned his head, gazing over the rooftops toward the sea. There were lights burning on Shadow Island too. Some down by the water, some high up on the walls. The towers and battlements were silhouetted against the paler backdrop of the skyline. It was dark all along the coast, but Shadow Island seemed somehow much blacker than anything else. Max looked at its somber outline and felt a shiver run through his body. He quickly pulled the shutters closed and moved away from the window. It was just an island.

He threw back the sheet and climbed into bed. He already had a schedule in his head of what he was going to do the next day, and he was impatient to begin. Sleep seemed a waste of valuable time. Still, in just a few minutes he had fallen into a deep sleep.

He was woken by the noise of a car tooting its horn and loud Spanish voices outside on the street. Max didn't know what they were saying, but he knew he wasn't going to get back to sleep again. He washed quickly and went down to the dining room.

Consuela wasn't up yet, so he ate breakfast alone— rolls and Coca-Cola, the only drink on offer apart from tea and coffee, neither of which Max liked. He was spreading apricot jam on his third roll when Consuela walked in. Well, "walked" was something of an under- statement. Consuela always made an entrance. This morning she was wearing a vivid crimson blouse, open at the throat, with a black skirt and sandals. There were only two other people in the room—a couple of men who looked like junior company executives—but they stopped eating and gaped at her as she went past their table to join Max.

The waiter was at her side so quickly he might have popped up through the floor in a puff of smoke. He pulled out a chair for her and fussed around, rearranging the cutlery and brushing breadcrumbs off the tablecloth.

"*Buenos días, señorita*. And what can I get you for breakfast?"

"Just coffee, please," Consuela replied, smiling graciously at the waiter, who flushed with pleasure and scurried away to the kitchen. "You're up early," she said to Max.

"I wanted to get going. How did you sleep?"

"Fine. You?"

"Not too bad. You want one of these rolls?"

Consuela shook her head. "So what are you planning to do first?"

"Go and see this lawyer, Estevez. Find out what he's doing on Mum's case."

"And then?"

"We'll see. Let's concentrate on one thing at a time."

Alfonso Estevez's office was in the center of Rio Verde, tucked away down a dark, narrow side street in an old

Spanish colonial building with a red-tiled roof and an ornate wrought-iron balcony outside the second-floor window. There was an outer office occupied by a swarthy middle-aged secretary wearing glasses and a shapeless black dress.

Señor Estevez was engaged with another client, she informed Max and Consuela, but if they wished to come back later, he might possibly see them then. Max wasn't going to be fobbed off with excuses, not after they'd flown five thousand miles to be there. He said they'd wait and plonked himself down on a chair, Consuela next to him. The secretary didn't argue but returned to reading the magazine she had open on her desk.

Max looked around. The office was far from impressive. The floor was dirty, the paint on the walls was peeling, and in one corner the plaster was so damp it had fallen away in chunks. Flies buzzed in through the open window and crawled lazily across the furniture. There was an atmosphere of idleness about the place. The secretary clearly didn't have any work to do, and even the ceiling fan seemed to be turning very slowly, as if it couldn't be bothered to keep the room cool. None of it filled Max with confidence in the lawyer who had been entrusted with his mother's legal affairs.

A full half hour went by before the inner door

opened and a young woman in a short skirt, tight top, and stiletto-heeled boots emerged. She said something in Spanish to the secretary and flounced out into the street.

"Is he going to see us now?" Consuela asked.

The secretary shrugged. "Soon."

Another five minutes went by. And another. And another. Max had waited long enough. "This is ridiculous," he said. He strode over to the inner door, threw it open, and walked into the lawyer's office.

Alfonso Estevez was leaning back in his chair with his feet on the desk, a cigar smoldering in one hand and a large glass of rum clutched in the other. He started in surprise and stared at Max. *"¿Quién eres tú?"* he asked.

Max understood enough of the language to know what Estevez had said. "I'm Max Cassidy," he replied in English.

"Uh?"

"You're my mother's lawyer. Or had you forgotten?"

Consuela came in behind Max. Estevez looked at her and hurriedly removed his feet from his desk. He put the glass he was holding down out of sight on the floor, but the smell of rum still filled the room.

"Did you make appointment?" the lawyer asked, speaking in English now.

"Why, are you *busy*?" Max said. He sat down opposite Estevez and glared at him. The lawyer was in his forties, a dark-skinned, fleshy man with a thick curving mustache.

"I don't know you coming," Estevez said. He smiled at Max, revealing yellowish teeth and a lot of gold fillings. "You no tell me."

"I want to talk about my mother," Max said.

"Yes, of course, your mother. How is she?"

"She's in prison," Max said bluntly. "Aren't you supposed to be getting her out?"

Estevez frowned. He wasn't used to being spoken to so directly, especially by a teenage boy. "Yes, I trying," he said defensively.

"Are you?"

"Listen, Max, you are young. You not understand how these things work."

"I understand enough to know when I'm being ripped off."

"What?"

Consuela put her hand on Max's arm. "Easy now," she said softly. "Don't get angry—it won't help."

She addressed Estevez in Spanish that was too fast for

Max to follow. The lawyer replied and then Consuela snapped back at him, her tone sharp.

Estevez shrugged. "Your mother's case," he said to Max, reverting to English, "it is complicated. I am doing everything I can."

"Oh, yes?" Max said. "And what might that be?"

Estevez waved his cigar in the air. "The law, it is very slow. Things take time in Santo Domingo. It not like England here."

"Okay, so tell me exactly how things stand at the moment," Max said.

"There is a lot of paperwork to prepare for the appeal. Documents for the court."

"Has a date been set for the hearing?"

"Not yet."

"Is it going to be set soon?"

"Who knows? That depends on the judge."

"We've been waiting two years already. How much longer is it going to be?"

"That is impossible to say. Two, three years, maybe longer."

"Three years?" Max exclaimed. "My mum has to stay in jail for another three years before her appeal is even heard?"

"Three years is not long time."

"It is to my mum," Max exploded. "And it is to me. *Three years!*"

"Can nothing be done to speed it up?" Consuela asked.

Estevez sucked hard on his cigar, then puffed smoke into the air. "Is possible," he said.

"What do you mean?" Consuela said.

"I mean, is possible if we make arrangement with judge."

"You mean bribe him?" snapped Max.

"No, no, is not a bribe. It is arrangement fee. There is difference."

"And how much would this fee be?" Max said.

"I don't know. Ten thousand dollars. Twenty."

"Twenty thousand dollars? Are you serious?"

"Is serious business," Estevez replied. "Your mother is convicted of murder. To get off murder conviction cost big money."

"But she's *innocent*," Max said.

Estevez looked puzzled by this remark. "What difference that make?" he said. "She in jail. She want to get out, she have to pay."

"What kind of stupid legal system have you got here?"

"That how things work in Santo Domingo. You pay

judge, you get appeal hearing. You no pay, you wait."

"And all the money we've been paying you?" Max said. "What's happened to that?"

"That for my expenses. For work I do," Estevez said.

"What work?"

"Eh?"

Max pushed back his chair and stood up. He turned to Consuela. "Let's go, we're getting nowhere here." He headed for the door.

"Hey," Estevez called after him. "What you do? You want me to make arrangement, or not?"

Max ignored him. He walked out through the secretary's office and into the street.

Consuela hurried after him. "Max, wait!"

Max kept going. Only when they were well away from the lawyer's office did he stop. He leaned back on the wall of a building and let out a deep breath, trying to calm himself down.

"Sometimes you're so impetuous," Consuela said. "Estevez is your mother's lawyer."

"He's a liar and a crook," said Max.

"We need him."

"For what? He's taken our money for two years and done nothing at all for it. It's over."

"You're firing him?"

"You bet I am."

"Max, don't be rash. Without a lawyer, how are you going to help your mother?"

"Having a lawyer hasn't helped her so far, has it? He's just milking us dry. You saw him. He's nothing but an idle drunk."

"But he knows the system here. We don't."

"If I thought it would make a difference, I'd find twenty thousand dollars to bribe the judge. I'd find fifty, a hundred thousand, if I could be sure it would get Mum out of prison. But it won't. Estevez will take the money for himself, or the judge will take it but then demand more to let her off."

"What alternative do we have?" Consuela said.

"Mum's in England, not Santo Domingo. We cut the Santo Domingo courts out of it," Max said. "We find evidence to show conclusively that she didn't kill my dad and we take it to an English court. They'll have to listen to us, and if they don't, we'll go to the press, the media, and make a fuss until they do."

"And where are we going to find this evidence?"

"I don't know," Max said. "But I know where we have to begin looking."

8

THE TWO ARMED GUARDS AT THE ENTRANCE to the Playa d'Oro holiday resort were big men in khaki uniforms and heavy combat boots. They were private security officers, but they looked like soldiers. They wore wraparound sunglasses and peaked caps over short army-style haircuts, and cradled in their arms were gleaming semiautomatic rifles.

The taxi that brought Max and Consuela out from Rio Verde stopped at the checkpoint. One of the guards leaned down to ask for their passports. As he did so, his eyes flicked around the interior of the taxi before scrutinizing the occupants. Max got just a cursory glance, but Consuela was subjected to a long, lingering inspection.

"British?" the guard said, studying Max's passport.

"Yes."

"And Spanish?"

"Yes," Consuela replied.

"You are staying here?" the guard asked.

"Just visiting for the day."

The guard took their passports over to the hut beside the checkpoint and entered their details on a computer. While he was doing this, his colleague checked the trunk of the taxi and ran a mirror on a stick along the ground to check the underside of the car. Some of the richest people in the world stayed at Playa d'Oro. And rich people expected the highest security.

The first guard came back out of the hut. He returned the passports to Consuela and handed her two day passes.

"You must give these back on your way out," he instructed them.

The steel barrier blocking the road rose silently into the air, allowing the taxi through. The contrast with the world outside the resort was immediately apparent. The road from Rio Verde had been rough and full of potholes, the land beside it brown and dusty. In the shantytown in the suburbs, skinny, malnourished children had played barefoot beside open sewers. But here in Playa d'Oro the road was smooth and spotlessly clean as if it were scrubbed with disinfectant every night. There were beautiful landscaped gardens on one side— rolling lawns and flower beds packed with luxuriant tropical flowers; on the other side was a golf course with velvety fairways and greens broken up by small shimmering lakes and bunkers of pure white sand.

Ahead of them, half a mile in the distance, was the resort complex—a huge fifteen-story hotel, a domed casino, restaurants and shops—and the theater where Max's father had performed for the last time. The buildings were spread out over a broad plain just behind the golden beach—it looked more like a small town than a holiday resort.

"Wow!" he said. "I've never seen anything like it."

"It's quite something, isn't it?" Consuela agreed. "It's so big there's a shuttle bus to take guests from one end to the other. Some people live here all year round. They never have to leave. Everything they could possibly want is provided."

The taxi stopped outside the main entrance to the hotel. A porter in a crisp green-and-gold uniform stepped forward and whipped open the rear door of the taxi for Max and Consuela to climb out.

"Good morning, madam, sir. Welcome to Playa

d'Oro," he said in English. He was Santo Domingan, but English was the main language of Playa d'Oro, as most of the guests were American or European. "Do you have any luggage?"

"No, we're just visiting," Consuela replied.

"The visitors' information desk is just inside the hotel lobby. Enjoy your time at Playa d'Oro."

Consuela paid the taxi driver and they watched him drive back toward the exit.

"Where do you want to go first?" asked Consuela.

"Show me where Mum and Dad stayed," Max said.

The bungalows were near the beach. To get there they had to walk past one of the resort's many cafés and swimming pools. The pool was almost the size of a soccer field, the terrace covered with lounge chairs on which bronzed guests in swimsuits were sunbathing. Waiters in white uniforms moved back and forth from the café, delivering drinks and snacks.

"It's a nice life, if you can afford it," Consuela said dryly.

"It looks boring to me," Max replied. "Just lying around frying in the sun."

The path dropped away from the terrace through a shady grove of palm trees and shrubs before emerging beside a cluster of straw-roofed wooden bungalows, each

119

with its own veranda and patch of garden. Consuela showed Max the one where his parents had stayed.

"They each have a double bedroom, a bathroom, a sitting room, and a small kitchenette."

"Where did *you* stay?" Max asked.

"I was up in the main hotel building. Your father was a celebrity. That's why they gave him one of these beach places."

Max studied the bungalows. There must have been forty or fifty of them, but they were well spread out among palm trees and lawns so each one had some privacy.

"And the rocks where my dad's stuff was found . . . ?" he asked.

"Down here."

Max followed Consuela farther along the path to the top of the beach and a cluster of jagged black rocks.

"His jacket was dumped about there," she said, pointing. "His wallet was just beside it. His money and credit cards were still inside. That's why the police ruled out robbery as a motive for his murder."

"If he *was* murdered," Max said. "And the knife?"

"It was down there, in that crack between the rocks. I didn't get a close look—the police cordoned the area off immediately."

Max crouched down and peered into the crack. There

seemed something peculiar, creepy even, about what he was doing: examining the scene where his mother was alleged to have killed his father. He'd imagined it so many times. Now that he was actually here, he was struck by how similar it was to what he'd pictured.

He straightened up and looked around, trying to visualize what it had been like that night. There were lights along the path, but none on the beach. It would have been dark. The nearest bungalow was fifty yards away. It was easy to understand why no guests had heard or seen anything unusual that night.

"And those are the boats over there?" Max asked.

"Yes."

"Were they that far away at the time?"

"Yes, that's pretty much where they were."

They walked along the beach toward the boats. The sand was dry and soft. Consuela removed her sandals and went barefoot.

The boats were pulled up above the high-tide line. Some were small sailing dinghies, others were rowboats with their oars stored inside across the slatted seats. Max gripped the edge of one of the rowboats and heaved. It moved a couple of inches and then ground to a halt in the sand.

"So let's get this straight," he said. "According to the police and the prosecution in the court case, my mum killed my dad over there, then dragged his body all the way along the beach. That's . . . what? About eighty yards? My dad was six feet tall and must have weighed a hundred and eighty pounds. My mum's five foot five and maybe a hundred and twenty pounds. She then supposedly lifted my dad's body into a rowboat, single-handedly dragged the boat down to the water, and rowed out to sea to dump his body. I don't believe a word of it. Could you have dragged a man's body that far?"

Consuela thought for a minute. "No, I don't think so."

"And the boat. You try pulling it."

Consuela hooked her hands over the edge of the rowboat and pulled back with all her strength. The boat didn't move even an inch.

"How do guests get the boats into the water?" Max said.

"There's a hut over there—you see it? There are two attendants on duty during the day. They put the boats in the sea. But they don't work at night."

"Have you got the camera?"

Consuela rummaged in her shoulder bag and handed Max the small digital camera they'd brought with them. He snapped a few shots of the area, showing the size of the boats and their position in relation to the rocks. Then he turned to face the sea. The beach shelved quite steeply. Angry white-capped waves were rolling in and breaking on the sand with a thunderous roar. You'd have to be a confident swimmer to go out into the surf. Not that there were many swimmers in the water. At Playa d'Oro, if you wanted to swim, you used one of the hotel pools. The sea was far too wild for most of the guests. It had waves, seaweed, creatures lurking at the bottom—and no waiters to bring out your drinks.

"The police sent divers down, didn't they?" Max said. "To look for Dad's body?"

"Just one, I believe," Consuela answered. "The Santo Domingo police only have one diver. And I don't think he looked very far."

Max scanned the coastline. There were a few rocks out in the middle of the bay and, away to the south beyond the headland, the distinctive outline of Shadow Island. But there was an awful lot of open water. If a body had been dumped out there, the chances of finding it were minuscule.

Max took a few more photos. "What do *you* think really happened?" he said to Consuela.

He'd asked her that question a lot over the past two

years, but Consuela never committed herself to a defi-
nite answer. "You know I don't know, Max."

"But if you had to speculate. Now you're back here
and can see the area again."

Consuela gave a slight shrug. "It had to have been a
man—maybe more than one—who dragged or carried
your father's body that distance. Not many women—
and certainly not your mother—could have done it."

"And their motive?"

"I don't know."

"Not robbery, we know that. Why would anyone
have wanted to kill Dad?" Max looked out across the
sea again. A small fishing boat was chugging back to
Rio Verde. It was close enough to the shore for him
to see the skipper at the wheel, a second man lounging
back in the stern.

"You think Dad's body is somewhere out there?"

"Don't think about such things, Max," Consuela said
with a shudder. She watched him discreetly, to see how
he was taking all this. She'd been opposed to coming
to Santo Domingo, but maybe it was a good thing for
Max to be here now. Maybe it would help him come
to terms with what had occurred.

"That's what we're here for," Max said. "To think
about Dad, to figure out what happened to him."

He had prepared himself for this moment. For his visit to the last place his father had been seen alive, the place where most people—maybe everybody except Max—believed he had been killed. It was such a beautiful, idyllic spot. The idea that his father had died here was horrific. Was it true? Had he really been killed just a few yards away from where Max was standing now? And was his body really out there in the depths of the ocean?

He had been coping well up till now. He'd focused on the business at hand—examining the area where it had all happened, getting a feel for the location. But now that he'd done that, his mind was starting to dwell on his emotions. He was picturing what might have taken place, seeing his father's face again, and it upset him. Suddenly, he didn't want to be there anymore. He wanted to get far away from Playa d'Oro.

"Let's go," he said abruptly. "I've had enough of this place."

9

SEEING THE FISHING BOAT OUT ON THE SEA
had suddenly reminded Max of something. Alexander
Cassidy had chartered a boat during his stay in Santo
Domingo and gone out fishing. Max had never known
his father to take the slightest interest in fishing. Boats
had never appealed to him either. He'd been a bad
sailor, seasick even when it was calm, and the waters
off Santo Domingo were anything but calm.

What had his mum said at Levington Prison on
Sunday? Max's dad had wanted to get away from
Playa d'Oro, so he'd gone into Rio Verde and hired a
boat at the harbor. He'd hired the boat's captain, too.
Fernando Gonzales.

In the afternoon, after he and Consuela had returned

to their hotel, Max went looking for Fernando Gonzales. Consuela didn't go with him. Something—maybe the long flight from Britain, maybe the hotel food the night before—had upset her stomach. Like most of the population of Rio Verde, she had retired to her room for a siesta. It was baking hot outside, and the locals knew better than to venture out into the midday sun. But Max didn't want to stay inside and rest.

Leaving his room key at reception, he went out into the city. The streets were quiet. There was very little traffic. All the shops and offices had closed for a few hours, leaving only a handful of restaurants and bars open. He walked down the hill. Max didn't have a map of Rio Verde, but he knew that if he kept going downhill, sooner or later he'd have to arrive at the harbor.

The city had been built in tiers up the hillside next to the river. Large parts of it—particularly the Old Town, where the Hotel San Rafael was located—predated the invention of the motorcar. The streets running horizontally along the slope were narrow, intended for horse-drawn carts or donkeys, and the streets running vertically weren't really streets at all—they were steep alleys, many of them simply long flights of twisting steps.

Max went down one set of steps, then another. The high buildings on either side blocked out the sun, but even so it was unpleasantly hot and humid. After a few minutes, Max could feel sweat running down his back, and he wondered whether he might have been better off staying in the hotel with Consuela and having a siesta.

He came to a T junction, where a street cut across his path from right to left. On the far side was an uninterrupted line of houses and shuttered shops. To keep going down the hill he'd have to turn left or right and look for a break in the buildings, maybe another flight of steps. But which way to go?

He turned right and almost immediately realized he'd made a mistake. The street was starting to veer *up* the hill. He turned and went back the way he'd come. As he reached the steps he'd walked down only seconds earlier, a man burst out in front of him, obviously in a hurry. Max couldn't stop in time. The two of them collided.

"*¡Perdón!*" Max said, using one of his few words of Spanish.

"What?" the man exclaimed in English. "Oh, sorry."

Max stepped back and saw who it was: Derek Pratchett. The salesman was red in the face and sweating heavily. His cheeks and forehead were dripping, and there were damp patches under the arms of his shirt.

"I say, what a surprise. Fancy bumping into you. *Literally* bumping into you." Pratchett gave a feeble laugh. "You're not hurt, are you?"

"No, I'm fine," Max said.

"What're you doing down here?"

"Just exploring."

"It's like a maze, isn't it? Nothing seems to go in a straight line."

"And you?" Max asked. "Where are you going?"

"Me? Well . . ." Pratchett seemed flustered. He had to think for a moment. "I've got a meeting. I'm looking for the Calle Something-or-other. These Spanish street names are so hard to remember, aren't they? I know it's around here somewhere. Must go. See you about."

Pratchett scurried away, but Max stayed where he was for a few minutes. Had that encounter been an accident? Or had Pratchett been following him? Max was on his guard now. As he descended the next flight of steps, he looked back continually, but he saw no sign of the salesman.

Nor did he notice the small, inconspicuous man in a white shirt who gave him a moment to turn the corner before coming down the steps behind him.

Max stayed vigilant when he reached the harbor, pausing to look around carefully before he went in search of Fernando Gonzales. There were two sections to the harbor—the older, smaller part that had a stone quay with local fishing boats moored alongside it, and a newer, larger part that was the marina for the yachts and cabin cruisers of Santo Domingo's wealthy visitors.

Max walked past the marina. The boats tied to the wooden jetties were uniformly large and luxurious, but they were nothing compared to those moored farther out in the river. Those vessels were like mini–cruise ships—sleek and streamlined, with berths for a dozen or more people. Their owners were sitting on deck beneath striped awnings, eating lunches prepared by their on-board chefs and served by uniformed waiters. Max could hear the faint clink of cutlery, the tinkle of champagne glasses, and laughter drifting across the estuary.

At the mouth of the river, in the wide channel between the mainland and Shadow Island, the largest, most impressive boat of all was anchored. It must have been at least twice the size of its nearest rival—two hundred fifty feet or more, with portholes along the sides and a helipad and helicopter on the stern deck.

Beside these floating palaces, the boats belonging to the local fishermen looked scruffy and forlorn. Actually, most of them *were* scruffy and forlorn. Their wooden hulls were scratched and patched with tar, their cabins faded and weathered by the sun and the salt. One or two looked so old and fragile, it was a wonder they were still floating, never mind being used for fishing in the fierce waters off the Santo Domingo coast.

A gnarled-looking fisherman in a dirty shirt and oily jeans was repairing a net on the quayside, his face shaded from the sun by a wide-brimmed hat. Max went up to him and said politely, *"¿Habla inglés?"*

The fisherman looked up. His skin had the color and texture of old leather. "English? A little," he said.

"I'm looking for a man named Fernando Gonzales. He has a boat."

The fisherman frowned, his whole face wrinkling. "Fernando? He no here. He dead."

"He's *dead*?" Max said. "When did he die?"

The fisherman shook his head vaguely. "One, two year ago." He bent over his work, his fingers expertly sewing up a tear in his net.

"Did he have any family?" Max asked.

"Yes, family."

"Do you know where they live?"

The fisherman gestured up the hill. "That way. Calle San Miguel. Number three."

Max thanked him and walked away, heading for the steps up the hill.

He was out of sight of the harbor, behind a row of houses, when the small man in the white shirt crossed the quay, flashed his police badge at the fisherman, and started questioning him.

Calle San Miguel was in the lower part of the Old Town, just above the harbor. There were no grand colonial houses here, no open squares. The buildings were shabby and rundown, packed closely together around dark courtyards. Signs of poverty and neglect were everywhere—broken shutters, boarded-up windows, missing tiles on roofs, children in ragged clothes playing games in the narrow, litter-strewn streets.

Max took a while to find number three. He went through a brick archway into a courtyard enclosed by tall, dilapidated apartment blocks. Above him was a spider's web of washing lines strung between balconies, the dangling clothes almost blotting out the sky. An elderly woman dressed entirely in black was sitting out by her door, chewing on a crust of bread.

"Gonzales?" Max said to her.

The woman jabbed a finger into the air. *"Segundo piso."*

Segundo? Max thought. That meant "second." *Segundo piso* had to mean "second floor." He thanked the old lady and went up the open staircase to the next floor. He knocked on a door and waited.

The woman who answered was thin and scrawny, her face lined and careworn.

"Señora Gonzales?" Max said.

"Sí."

"Do you speak English?"

"¿Qué?"

"English. I'm sorry, I don't speak much Spanish."

The woman turned her head and called out a name: "Isabella!"

A girl about the same age as Max appeared in the hallway. She was tall and lithe in her jeans and T-shirt, her long black hair tied back in a ponytail. The woman said something to her in Spanish and she came to the door.

"I speak some English," she said. "What do you want?"

"To ask you a few questions," Max said.

The girl eyed him warily. "Questions about what? Who are you?"

"My name's Max Cassidy."

"Cassidy?"

Isabella seemed to recognize the name. She licked her lips and peered over Max's shoulder, checking the staircase behind him. "Like the one who disappear?" she said.

"That's right. Alexander Cassidy. He's my dad. Your father took him out fishing in his boat."

"Why you come here?" Her eyes flicked over his shoulder again.

"Can I come in?" Max said.

"What for?"

"I'm trying to find out what happened to him. I won't stay long. Please. Just a couple of minutes."

Isabella studied his face.

Max smiled at her. "I've come all the way from England."

She hesitated. "You are alone?"

"Yes."

"Not here. We go for walk."

Isabella said something to her mother and stepped out of the apartment, closing the door behind her. Max followed her down the stairs and back through the courtyard to the street. Isabella paused, looking around cautiously. Max could see she was on edge.

"What's the matter?"

"This way."

She led him along the street and through the remains of a doorway into a ruined building. They clambered over the mounds of rubble and sat on the stump of a brick wall. Max noticed that Isabella's jeans and T-shirt were faded and threadbare, and there were holes in the toes of her cheap sneakers.

"You remember my father?" Max asked.

"Everyone remember. Was in all the papers. Was big news. Famous Englishman disappear, police say wife kill him."

"My mother didn't kill him."

"No? But she . . . There was, what you call it? In courtroom."

"She was put on trial, yes," Max said. "And convicted. But she didn't kill him."

"Why you come to us?" Isabella asked. "We know nothing about it."

"I'm just curious. My dad wasn't interested in fishing. Why would he get your father to take him out?"

"My father take lot of tourists in his boat. Not all like fishing. Some just want trip on boat."

"My dad didn't like boats either. Did your father ever say anything to you about him?"

Isabella glanced nervously over her shoulder, looking back toward the street.

"Are you scared of something?" Max said.

"This not good thing to talk about. The police, they question my father after yours disappear. They question us too—my mother, my brothers and sisters and me—after Papa died. We no want trouble from police."

"I'm not here to make trouble. Do you know where they went that day?"

"Out to sea. That all I know."

"When did your father die?"

"Two years ago. June."

"June? The same month as my dad?"

"Yes. Was not long after."

She looked down. Max sensed that this was still a very painful subject for her.

"I'm sorry. Do you mind if I ask how he died?"

"He drown. He go out in boat and fall into sea. Another fisherman find his boat up the coast, no one on board."

"Was his body found?"

"Yes, it wash up on beach."

Max nodded sympathetically. Isabella turned her

head away, but not before he saw the gleam of moisture in her eyes.

"That must have been hard for you," he said. "How many brothers and sisters do you have?"

"There are five of us. Six with my mother. She work at night, as cleaner for offices in Rio Verde, but pay is not good. Without my father, it is hard. We try to sell his boat, but no one want. Boat is old, need a lot of work. And no one want to go fishing now. Is too hard, too dangerous. Young people, they all want job at Playa d'Oro. Is easier there, even if the pay is no better."

They were silent for a time. From where they were sitting, there was a clear view over the estuary toward Shadow Island. Waves broke over the rocks on the shore, and up on the battlements of the fortress a figure paced up and down like a guard on sentry duty.

"Did your father ever take tourists out there, to Shadow Island?" Max asked.

"Isla de Sombra? No," Isabella said. "You can't go there. Is private. They have a boat. You go near, men on boat tell you to go away."

"Really?"

"You get too close, they—I don't know how you say. They do this." Isabella held up her left hand, the fingers extended, and smashed her right fist hard into the palm.

"They ram you?" Max said.

"Yes, ram you. It happen once to my father. He get crack in boat, have to come back to harbor and mend it."

"That's pretty nasty. How can they get away with that kind of thing?"

"Man who own island, he is very rich, one of richest men in world. And very powerful. He do whatever he like."

"What's his name?"

"Señor Clark. Julius Clark. That's his boat out there. The big one with the helicopter."

"And Isla de Sombra is his holiday home?"

"I don't know what he do there. Not holiday. There other people on island. They work there."

"Doing what?"

"I don't know. They come into Rio Verde sometimes. Go to shops, to bar."

"Your father's death . . . ," Max said. "It was an accident?"

"That what police say. What else could it be?"

Max didn't reply. He was watching the figure on the battlements. More than ever now, it looked like a soldier on guard duty. The island seemed a strange place. A guard on the fortress, a boat patrolling the sea around it to keep people away . . . Max knew rich people liked to protect their privacy, but ramming boats that came too near seemed a bit extreme.

"Thanks for your help," he said.

"That all you want to know?"

"Yes."

Isabella turned to look at him. Her dark eyes were serious, her forehead wrinkling as if she were puzzled. "Why you ask me if my father's death was accident?"

"I have the feeling nothing is what it seems here," Max said.

It was late afternoon when Max returned to the Hotel San Rafael. He went upstairs to his room and splashed cold water on his face to cool himself down. Then he went next door to Consuela's room. She must still be having her siesta.

Max knocked on the door. He heard footsteps inside the room. The handle turned and the door swung open.

A woman peered out at him. But it wasn't Consuela.

She was older, a plump woman in her forties or fifties, with fat legs showing beneath her dress and grayish hair that had the texture of wire wool. *"¿Sí?"* she said.

Max stared at her. He'd never seen her before in his life. Maybe he'd somehow got the wrong room. But no, there was the number on the door. Max was in room four, Consuela in room five. So who was this woman? A cleaner, perhaps? Or another member of the hotel staff? That must be it. She was a hotel employee sent up to Consuela's room for some reason.

"Is Consuela here?" he asked.

"¿Qué?"

"Señorita Navarra."

"Who?" the woman said, speaking English now.

"Consuela Navarra. This is her room," Max said.

The woman shook her head. "No, this is my room."

Max craned his neck to see over the woman's shoulder. There was a single bed in the room, a bedside cabinet, and an old wooden wardrobe. But no Consuela.

"When did you arrive?" he asked.

"Arrive?" the woman repeated. "Today. This afternoon."

"Okay. I'm sorry to bother you."

Max walked away, frowning. Consuela must have moved rooms while he was out. It was odd that she hadn't left a note to let him know. He went downstairs to the foyer. There was a young woman Max hadn't seen before behind the reception desk. He asked her which room Consuela was in. She checked the register and gave Max a blank look.

"What was the name again?"

"Consuela Navarra," Max said.

"I'm sorry, but there is no Consuela Navarra staying in the hotel."

"There must be. Could you check again, please?"

The receptionist inspected the register once more. "Navarra?" she said.

"That's right."

"No. No Navarra."

"That's impossible," said Max. "She was in room five."

"Room five is occupied by a Señora Córdoba."

"But she's only just arrived. Before that it was Consuela's room. She checked in with me yesterday evening."

"Room five was not occupied last night."

"Of course it was. There must be a mistake in the register. We arrived together. What room is she in now?"

"I already tell you, señor," the receptionist said. "There is no Señorita Navarra in this hotel."

Max stared at her. What was going on? Was it a simple mix-up, a language problem? Did this woman not understand what he was saying?

"Can I see the register?" he asked.

The receptionist shrugged and turned the book round. Max studied the list of entries. There was his name—Max Cassidy—with his passport number, nationality, and room number next to it. But there was no mention of Consuela. The woman had been correct. According to the register, room five had been unoccupied the previous night.

Max felt a sudden flutter of anxiety in his stomach. Something wasn't right here. Why wasn't Consuela in the register? There had to be an explanation. Maybe someone had simply forgotten to write her name in the book. But that didn't make sense either. Max had *seen* her name being recorded when they arrived. He'd been standing next to Consuela when she'd handed her passport to the receptionist; he'd watched the woman write her name, and then his, in the book.

"Could I speak to the manager, please?" demanded Max.

"The manager?"

"Yes. Now."

The receptionist shrugged again and went through a door into an office at the back of the foyer. Max saw her talking to a man seated behind a desk. The man glanced sideways at Max through the door, then came out to the reception desk.

"You have a problem?" he said bluntly. He was a short, shifty-looking man with small eyes.

"Yes, I have a problem," Max replied. "I arrived yesterday evening with a woman—Consuela Navarra. She spent last night in room five, but she's not there now. Another woman is in the room, and your receptionist tells me you have no record of Consuela ever being here."

The manager pulled the register across the desk and examined it closely. "You are Señor Cassidy, no?"

"Yes."

"You must be mistaken, Señor Cassidy. We have no Señorita Navarra staying here."

"But that's ridiculous," Max said. "She was here last night. Ask your receptionist who was on duty yesterday. She had breakfast with me in the dining room this morning. Check with your waiters."

"I repeat, señor, there is no Señorita Navarra in the hotel. Maybe you imagined her."

"'Imagined her'?" Max snapped. "What are you talking about? She's here. I know she is. I want to check all the rooms."

"That is not possible, señor."

Imagined her? What kind of stupid remark was that? What were these people doing? What had happened to Consuela? Had she been kidnapped? Or was she still somewhere in the hotel? Max was going to find out.

He spun on his heel and dashed up the stairs to the second floor. Behind him, the manager called out for him to stop, but Max took no notice. He tried the first door he came to. It was locked. The second door wasn't. Max threw it open and looked around. The room was empty. He moved on down the corridor, checking all the unlocked rooms. When he walked into room five, Señora Córdoba was lying on her bed reading a book.

"Excuse me," Max said. He glanced around, then pulled open the wardrobe doors.

"Hey, what you do?" Señora Córdoba protested.

Max riffled through the clothes hanging in the wardrobe. None of them were Consuela's. They were too drab, too dowdy. The shoes on the floor of the wardrobe weren't hers either. They were square and clumpy like hiking boots. Consuela wouldn't have been seen dead in them.

Señora Córdoba was on her feet now, shouting at Max in Spanish. He ignored her and pulled out the drawers of the bedside cabinet. They were all empty. There was nowhere else to search, so Max headed for the door. As he stepped into the corridor, the manager, accompanied by another man, grabbed hold of him. The second man was big and powerful. From the pungent aroma of fish and garlic that came off him, Max guessed he worked in the hotel kitchen.

"It's the police for you," the manager snapped furiously.

"Where's Consuela?" Max yelled. "What have you done with her?"

He struggled to escape, but the men were too strong for him. They picked him up and carried him downstairs.

10

THE HEAVY STEEL DOOR SLAMMED SHUT AND a key turned in the lock. Max looked around the tiny police cell. It was only about six feet square, with green mold on the walls and a bare earth floor. There was a low wooden platform at one side for prisoners to sleep on and a barred window high up the rear wall. The room smelled of damp and something sour like sweat or vomit. A cockroach scurried out from beneath the bed and away through a crack in the wall. Max shuddered. He'd never been anywhere so vile before.

He went to the back wall and stood underneath the window. Bending his knees, he leaped upward, grabbing hold of the bars over the window, then pulling himself up. The view wasn't worth the effort. There was nothing to see except a narrow alley and a brick wall.

Max dropped back down and paced across the floor like the caged animal he was. Anger was still simmering inside him. How dare they do this! How dare they arrest him and throw him in this stinking cell when he'd done nothing wrong! *Nothing wrong?* He almost laughed. What did right or wrong count for in Santo Domingo? His mother had done nothing wrong, and look what they'd done to her.

But underneath his anger he was worried. What had happened to Consuela? Where had she gone, and why was the hotel pretending that she'd never been there? And just as worrying, what was going to happen to him now? He was locked up in a filthy cell five thousand miles from home in a country where he had no friends, didn't know his rights, and couldn't speak the language. He dwelled on these questions for an hour or more before he heard a key in the lock and the cell door swung open. A police officer in a crumpled uniform beckoned him out. Max followed the man along a corridor and up a flight of stairs to the second floor of the police station. The officer knocked on a door and, when a deep voice from within called out,

"Come," ushered Max inside.

"The prisoner, Colonel," the police officer said in Spanish, then bowed and left.

There was a man sitting at a desk on the far side of the room. He wore a smart green uniform with medal ribbons on the breast and a lot of gold braid at the shoulders and cuffs. "Come here," he ordered in English.

Max walked across the office. It was a huge room, thirty feet long, with French windows that opened onto a balcony at one side and a polished wooden floor that creaked as Max crossed it. His legs were shaking. He didn't know who this man was, but his voice alone was enough to terrify him.

"Stop there." The man lifted his head from some papers he was studying and fixed Max with a penetrating stare. He was big, with a broad chest and muscular arms that bulged beneath the sleeves of his uniform. He had cropped black hair, dark stubble along his jawline, and a long ugly scar on his left cheek that looked like a knife wound. But it was his eyes Max noticed most. This man had the darkest, most frightening eyes Max had ever seen.

"My name is Colonel Pablo de los Mantequillas," he said. "I am the chief of police for Rio Verde."

Max swallowed but didn't say anything. Colonel Mantequillas didn't look like a man who engaged in idle small talk. He asked questions, and you answered those questions. Or else.

"I understand you have been causing trouble at the Hotel San Rafael," the police chief said. "We don't like foreign tourists who come here and make trouble."

"I wasn't making trouble," Max said.

"Be quiet!" Colonel Mantequillas's voice was like a whip crack. "You speak when I tell you and not before. You are not in England now. We do things differently in Santo Domingo, and you'd better not forget that. You were making trouble. Upsetting the guests and disrupting the efficient running of the hotel. Those are serious offenses."

Serious offenses? Max thought. *Upsetting a hotel guest? What kind of a country is this?* He was tempted to argue but thought better of it.

"What is this absurd story you told the hotel manager?" the police chief went on. "Something about a woman named"—he glanced at the papers on his desk—"Consuela Navarra. Explain yourself."

"It's not a 'story,'" Max said, his voice cracking with nerves.

"No?"

"I came to Santo Domingo with her. And then this afternoon—"

"Yes, I know what happened this afternoon," the

police chief interrupted. "There is not a shred of truth in what you say. There is no such woman as Consuela Navarra."

"But there is," Max said. "She traveled from England with me. I live with her in London. She was in the room next to me at the hotel. Ask the staff."

"We have. My men have made inquiries at the San Rafael. All the employees say you came alone."

"What? But that's rubbish. We checked in together, we had breakfast together. Did you ask the waiter who served us? Or the other guests? There were two men in the dining room. They saw Consuela."

"We have questioned all the staff. None of them has seen this woman you claim was with you. There is no mention of her in the hotel register."

"Someone must have changed the register," Max said.

"And why would anyone do that?" Colonel Mantequillas asked.

"I don't know. But she was with me, I swear." A thought came to him suddenly, and his hopes rose. "We had our passports examined at the airport when we arrived. Check with the airport. They'll have a record of Consuela."

"We already have. There is no record of a Consuela

Navarra entering the country."

"But that's—"

"Silence! You've made the whole thing up."

"No, I—"

"I said *silence!*" The police chief's dark, piercing eyes bored into Max's face. Max felt his skin go cold and he had to look away. "Why are you here?" Colonel Mantequillas demanded. "Why did you come to Santo Domingo?"

Max said nothing.

"Answer me!" the police chief snapped. "Why are you here?"

"To see my mother's lawyer. You must know about my mother."

"Oh, yes, we know all about your mother," Mantequillas sneered. "A convicted murderess. A woman who killed her own husband."

Max wasn't going to allow that to go unchallenged, however frightened he was of the police chief. "That's not true," he said forcefully. "She didn't kill my dad."

The colonel's eyes narrowed. "Are you calling me a liar, boy?"

"No, no," Max said hurriedly. "But there are—" He stopped, biting his lip. It didn't seem wise to go on.

"Yes?" the police chief said. "There are what?"

151

"Nothing," Max said.

"There are reasons to doubt her guilt? Is that what you were going to say?"

"Sort of," Max admitted.

"And these reasons, what are they?"

Max hesitated. But why not go on? Why not tell the chief of police what his force had got wrong?

"What they said happened that night can't have been right," Max said. "My mum couldn't have dragged my dad's body all that way along the beach. She couldn't have pulled the rowboat down to the water. She's not strong enough."

"You're saying my officers are incompetent? That their investigation was flawed?"

"Yes."

Max braced himself for another sharp reprimand, or worse, but the police chief merely laughed. A low, chilling laugh that made Max shiver.

"You have some nerve, boy, I'll give you that," Mantequillas said.

"I've seen where it supposedly happened. I've been to the beach, looked at the rowboats."

"So you've been snooping around Playa d'Oro, have you?"

"Why shouldn't I go there?" Max said defiantly. "Or

is that a serious offense here too?" he added rashly.

"Careful, boy," Colonel Mantequillas growled. "Don't push me too far."

"I want the case reopened," Max said, undeterred by the police chief's tone. "My mum's innocent. And *I* want a lawyer. You can't lock me up like this. I've done nothing wrong."

"You've wasted your trip, I'm afraid. The case will not be reopened. As far as the Santo Domingo police and the Santo Domingo courts are concerned, the case is solved. We caught the right person and she has been duly punished. Nothing you say will make us change our minds."

"But you're wrong," Max said fiercely. "You have to look at it again."

"Don't tell me what I *have* to do. Face the facts, boy. Your mother is guilty and will be in jail for the next eighteen years. You think about that on your flight home tomorrow."

"I'm not going home tomorrow."

"Oh, yes you are. You'll be taken back to your hotel now and confined to your room. In the morning you will be put on a flight to Miami, and from there to London."

"You can't do that," Max protested.

"I am the police chief of Rio Verde. I can do anything I like here." Colonel Mantequillas pressed the intercom on his desk and spoke to someone in rapid Spanish. Moments later, the door opened and two uniformed police officers came in.

"What about Consuela?" Max said quickly. "I have to find out what's happened to her."

"Consuela Navarra does not exist." The colonel glanced at the two officers. "Take him away."

The officers took hold of Max and escorted him from the room.

The door had barely closed behind them when another door, to one side of the police chief's desk, opened and a short, plump man entered the office. He was wearing a dark-gray suit, a waistcoat, and a tie, and he looked hot and flushed, his face gleaming with perspiration. "My goodness," Rupert Penhall said. "It's sweltering in here. Haven't you people heard of air conditioning?"

"You don't like the heat, you should stay in London, Mr. Penhall," Mantequillas said acidly.

Penhall sat down in front of the desk and wiped his brow with a pink silk handkerchief. "I hope I won't have to stay long," he said. "You did well, Colonel. The boy was well and truly frightened."

The police chief grinned wolfishly. "Frightening people is my specialty," he said.

"You think he's found out anything?"

"Nothing we should worry about. He's just a child. What can he possibly do to harm us?"

Penhall pursed his fleshy lips. "He's tougher than he looks, you know. We shouldn't underestimate him."

The police chief waved a hand dismissively. "Pah, he knows nothing."

"He went out to Playa d'Oro. He's a bright kid. Everything he said about the beach and the boat was correct."

"So? What difference does that make? Whatever he does or says, he will get nowhere in Santo Domingo. And *you* will make sure he gets nowhere in England."

"He went somewhere else this afternoon, when my man, Pratchett, lost him. You should have questioned him about that."

"Fortunately my men are more efficient than yours. He went to see the Gonzales family."

"The fisherman's family? They know something?"

"They were questioned vigorously after we killed Gonzales. They know nothing about his activities. They won't be a problem."

"Keep a sharp eye on the boy, Colonel. He's brave,

determined, like his father."

"I have everything under control," the police chief said.

"What about the woman?"

"Consuela Navarra? She is no threat either."

"Where is she?"

"In a cell in the basement. After nightfall, I will have her taken out to the island."

Penhall gave a smile of satisfaction. "Good. They will know what to do with her."

11

MAX WAS BACK IN HIS ROOM AT THE HOTEL
San Rafael. The fear and anger he'd felt during his
interview with the police chief had gone. He'd made
sure of that. They were dangerous emotions that could
do nothing to help him. He was calmer now and clear-
headed. His thoughts were focused on one objective:
getting away from his police guards.

He sat back on his bed, propped up against a pillow,
and stared across the room at the wall. He was locked
in and he was being watched. He wasn't onstage now.
He had no props, no hidden keys to assist him. This
wasn't a show-business act, it was the real world.

After a few minutes he slid off the bed, padded quietly

over to the door and put his eye to the keyhole. There was a police officer stationed outside in the corridor, sitting on a chair facing Max's door. He looked wide-awake and alert. Max straightened up and crossed to the window. The hotel, like much of Rio Verde, was built in the Spanish colonial style. His room had two French windows that opened inward, giving access to a small balcony edged with a waist-high wrought-iron railing. Max stepped cautiously onto the balcony and peered out. There was another officer standing in a doorway on the far side of the street, his gaze fixed on Max's window.

Max retreated and sat back down on the bed. This wasn't going to be easy. But he couldn't allow himself to be put on a plane home in the morning. He had to find out what had happened to Consuela—and to his dad. He knew it wasn't a coincidence: There had to be a link between the two.

He looked around the room. The French windows and the door were the only ways in or out. There were no ventilation grilles, no skylights, no bathroom with its own separate exit. *Bathroom?* The San Rafael was a cheap, old-fashioned hotel. None of the rooms had en suite bathrooms, but there was a communal bathroom just along the corridor—and that had a window overlooking the rear of the building.

Max got to his feet. He went to the door and hammered on it. "Hey, you out there," he called.

"What you want?" the policeman in the corridor shouted back.

"The toilet. I need the toilet. Do you understand?"

There was a pause. Then a key scraped in the lock and the door opened.

"You want toilet?" the policeman asked.

"Yes."

Max wondered whether he could make a run for it; dodge round the copper and away down the corridor. But the policeman was watching him closely. He was a wiry man with an athletic build. He looked quick on his feet. Max knew he wouldn't outrun him.

"I come with you," the policeman said.

He grasped Max's elbow tightly and led him along the corridor to the bathroom. There was an ancient, stained enamel bath with a shower over it at one side of the room and a separate toilet stall at the other. The window was between the two, immediately above a grimy washbasin.

"I'll be all right," Max said. "You can wait outside in the corridor."

"No, I wait here." The policeman leaned back on

the bathroom wall and crossed his arms.

Max could see there was no point in pushing him further. The copper wasn't going to leave him alone for a second. He went into the stall and had a pee, then came out and washed his hands. The window was right in front of him now and it was already ajar. All Max had to do was push it wider, climb out, and drop the couple of yards to the ground. But before he could make his move, the policeman stepped forward to stand beside him.

"You finish?" he said.

"Yes, I've finished."

The policeman grabbed his elbow again and took him back to his room.

He slumped down onto his bed and heard the key turn in the lock. So much for that idea.

Escaping through the bathroom was out. So was any chance of evading the policeman. He seemed too smart to fall for a crude trick. That left the window as the only possible escape route, but there was still the policeman outside keeping watch.

Max thought hard. He pictured the front of the hotel. There was an entrance in the middle with windows on either side; above that were three stories of bedrooms, each with its own balcony. How far apart were the balconies? That was important.

Max went back over to the open window but dropped to the floor so the policeman in the street wouldn't see him. He snaked forward and poked out his head cautiously. The balcony of the adjoining room—now apparently Señora Córdoba's room—was two or three yards away. Max reckoned he could fling himself across that distance and grab hold of the iron railing around the balcony. But what good would that do? Even if the policeman in the street didn't see him—and that was unlikely—Max would still have to sneak past Señora Córdoba and out into the corridor—the same corridor in which the first policeman was standing guard. Could Max slip out of Señora Córdoba's room without the officer seeing him? He didn't think so. Going sideways across the front of the building wasn't going to work.

How about hanging by his arms and dropping to the ground? He was only on the third floor. It couldn't be more than ten feet to the street. But that seemed even less likely to succeed. The policeman at the front of the hotel would certainly catch him.

That left only one other option. Max would have to climb *up* the building. He twisted his head and looked upward. The underside of the balcony above his was about eight feet away. If he stood on the railing of his own balcony and stretched out his arms, he might just be able to pull himself up. But that had the same drawback as climbing down. The policeman in the street would see him and raise the alarm.

Max slithered back inside his room and weighed his options. He could remain where he was until morning and hope that a better opportunity to escape would present itself before the police got him to the airport and put him on the plane. But would such an opportunity arise? He'd be foolish to depend on it.

Going up was his only option. It didn't matter if the policeman in the street saw him climbing up the building. Seeing wasn't the same as catching. The officer might start yelling; he might run into the hotel to alert his colleague. But if Max moved fast enough, he had a chance of getting away. And Max could move very fast when he had to.

He checked his watch. It was nearly nine o'clock and it was dark outside, but Max knew he had to be patient; wait a few hours until the policemen began to get bored and sleepy. He had to catch them off guard.

He closed his eyes and tried to relax. He thought he was too tense to sleep, but he must have dozed off anyway because when he next looked at his watch it was nearly eleven o'clock. He went across to the window. The policeman was still in the doorway opposite the hotel. He was leaning against the wall, his face in shadow so Max couldn't see his eyes. Was he awake? Max had to assume he was.

He took a last look around his room. He had his passport and money in his pocket. Everything else—his spare clothes, his wash things—he'd have to leave behind. He stepped out onto the balcony. The policeman across the street didn't move. Max waited a few seconds, then clambered nimbly up onto the railing. He balanced on the narrow iron strip, one hand pressed against the wall to steady himself, and reached up with his other arm. His fingertips just brushed the underside of the balcony above. He glanced down across the street. The policeman was still motionless. *Maybe my luck's in and he's asleep,* Max thought.

He braced himself. This was the really dangerous bit, where all the skills of balance and agility that he'd practiced for his stage act would be crucial. If he misjudged this, he would plummet to the pavement below and break his neck. He took a deep breath and launched himself upward. He grabbed the railings of the balcony above and clung on. Max dangled in space for a moment, then swung his legs, hooking them through the gaps in the metal. Ten seconds later he had pulled himself up and was standing on the balcony.

It was at that exact instant that the policeman across the street saw him and started shouting.

Max moved rapidly. The French windows next to him were half open, presumably to let in the cool night air. Max dived through the gap and dashed across the room. A man was snoring in the bed, but he didn't wake up, even when Max unlocked the door and went out into the corridor. *Which way now?* Max thought. *Make up your mind. Quickly.* The main stairs were to his left, but they were too risky. That was the way the policemen would come. Was there a back staircase, or a fire escape? He didn't know, but surely there had to be. He turned right, running along the corridor and round a corner. It was a dead end—no staircase anywhere. Max swore. What now? He went back to the corner and peeped out. He could hear heavy thudding footsteps on the stairs, voices shouting in Spanish. The policemen were heading toward him. Max looked around. There were doors on either side of the corridor. Some were obviously bedrooms—they had numbers on them—but one was marked BAÑO. Bathroom. Max pushed open the door and ducked inside.

There was a window next to the bath. He whipped it open and looked out. He was two floors up, but a couple of yards below him was the sloping roof of an outbuilding on the ground floor. Max didn't hesitate. He scrambled through the window and lowered himself down the wall, hanging from the windowsill by his fingertips. His feet stopped before they reached the outbuilding. Max let go and dropped, praying that the roof was strong enough to take his weight. It was. He landed lightly and immediately twisted round, slithering down the tiles on his backside. At the edge of the roof he slowed and rolled over onto his stomach to lower himself down into the yard in front of the outbuilding.

As his feet touched the ground, he heard a shout above him and glanced up. One of the policemen was leaning out of the bathroom window, screaming at him to stop.

Max sprinted away across the yard. He turned into the alley at the side of the hotel—and ran straight into another policeman, a third officer who must have been watching the rear of the building. The man caught hold of him. Max felt cold steel on his skin as a pair of handcuffs was fastened around his wrists.

"No more games," the policeman said in a thick Spanish accent. He took Max by the arm and led him away.

12

THEY DIDN'T RETURN HIM TO HIS ROOM IN the hotel as Max had expected, but took him instead back to the central police station and put him in a cell. It wasn't the same cell as before, but it was more or less identical in layout—a small square box with a high barred window, a dirt floor, and a wooden platform for a bed. There was no mattress or pillow, just rough bare planks.

"What about the handcuffs?" Max asked the police officer who'd brought him in. "Aren't you going to take them off?"

"You big trouble," the policeman replied. "Handcuffs stay on."

"But you can't do that," Max protested. "How

am I supposed to sleep?"

"That your problem," the officer said and went out, locking the cell door behind him.

Max sat down on the wooden platform. He was furious with himself for allowing the police officers to catch him. He'd had a chance to get away, and he'd blown it. Now he was in an even worse situation than before. He was still a prisoner, but he didn't have the luxury of a hotel room and a proper bed.

He looked around the cell. It had the same green mold on the walls as the previous one, the same sour stench. No doubt there were cockroaches here, too. There was a light in the ceiling, a single bulb glowing dimly behind a wire-mesh cover. Max could see that it was going to be left on all night, making sleep even more difficult.

Sleep? he thought. *Why are you thinking about going to sleep? You've failed once, but that doesn't mean you should give up the fight, just lie down and let them send you home in the morning. You've got to find another way of escaping.*

He went across to the door and crouched down by the keyhole. He'd gotten a good look at the key when the police officer had unlocked the door. Now he examined the lock itself. It was a big, sturdy-looking mechanism, but Max was knowledgeable enough about locks to realize that it wasn't very sophisticated. It was an old model that had been designed more for show than effectiveness. The lock—and the massive key that came with it—gave an impression of strength, but it was actually a very crude piece of ironwork. The tumblers inside, which were turned by the key to pull back the bolt, would be simple to pick—if Max had something to pick them with.

He heard footsteps in the corridor outside. Two sets. Male footsteps—Max could tell from the heavy sound. They went past his door and stopped outside the adjoining cell. A key rattled in a lock and a door squeaked open. Max heard the footsteps coming back, the two sets as before. Only this time there was a third set accompanying them. Lighter footsteps—maybe a woman's? Definitely—there was the unmistakable click of heels on the stone flags of the corridor. A woman? Heels? Max's heart leaped. He took a chance. "Consuela?" he shouted through his door. "Consuela, is that you?"

"Max?" It was her voice. "Max, you must get—"

The words were choked off abruptly.

"Consuela?" Max yelled. "Are you okay? What's happening? Consuela?"

The footsteps got fainter and then faded away

altogether. Max hammered on the door of his cell with his fists. "Hey, let me out!" he shouted. "Do you hear me? You can't keep me locked up like this!'

He knew he was wasting his breath, but he had to release some of the frustration that had built up inside him. What the hell was going on? Consuela was alive, at least. That was a relief, but why was she being kept in a police cell and where were they taking her?

Max went across to the back wall of his cell. He reached up, his wrists still handcuffed together, then jumped, grabbing hold of the bars over the window. He pulled himself up and looked out. His previous cell window had faced an alley and a brick wall, but this one overlooked the floodlit yard at the rear of the police station.

Consuela was being led across the yard by two police officers. They were each holding one of her arms and were practically carrying her, her feet hardly touching the ground. She was struggling to escape, but she was no match for the men.

"Consuela!" Max yelled.

Consuela twisted her head round. "Max . . ."

She shouted something else. Max didn't quite catch what it was because one of the policemen cupped his hand over her mouth to gag her again. Then she was bundled into the back of a police car and driven away. Max watched the car turn onto the street before he let go of the bars and dropped back down to the floor of his cell.

What had Consuela called? He'd caught only a few words before the police officer had cut her off. But one of the words had sounded like *ironed. Ironed?* Why would Consuela shout that? Max thought about it for a while; then it suddenly dawned on him. It wasn't *ironed*, it was *island*. It had to be Shadow Island.

Max sat on the wooden platform. He'd sensed there was something sinister about Isla de Sombra from the moment he'd arrived in Rio Verde. Was that where Consuela was being taken, or did she have another reason for mentioning it? Either way, it must be important, and Max wasn't going to be of any use to her stuck in a police cell. He had to get out.

He held up his arms and examined the cuffs. He'd seen similar ones before. His father had built up a vast collection of handcuffs and manacles, and Max had practiced escaping from every single one of them. These were British-made, but they were at least ten years old, and the lock on them—by modern standards—was flimsy. With the right tool, Max could have had them open in a few seconds. But he didn't have *any* tools on him, let alone the right one.

Maybe he could open them some other way. There were certain locks that could be disabled by tapping them in a particular place. Harry Houdini, the legendary escape artist, had kept a metal plate strapped to his leg underneath his trousers on which he could tap handcuffs to open them. But that was in the early twentieth century, and lock technology had moved on a lot since then. Still, it was worth a try.

Max shuffled to the end of the wooden platform and positioned his handcuffs so that the lock was directly in front of the sharp corner. He struck the cuffs against the wood several times, hoping the impact might dislodge the tumblers inside the lock. But nothing happened. What other method could he try?

Then he remembered. He was wearing trousers with a belt. And on the belt was a metal buckle. He reached down and unfastened it, then flipped out the metal spike in the center of the buckle and inserted it into the keyhole of the handcuffs. It wasn't the ideal implement for picking a lock, but it was more than adequate in Max's skilled hands. The lock clicked open. He pulled off the cuffs and rubbed his wrists, sore where the steel bands had chafed his skin.

Now for the door. Max crossed the cell and paused,

checking there was no guard outside who might hear him working on the lock. "Hello?" he called. "Is there anybody there?" He put his eye to the keyhole. "*Hola!*"

He saw nothing, heard no sound in the corridor. There was obviously no guard. That didn't surprise him. As far as the police were concerned, he was just a kid, a kid who was handcuffed and locked in a secure cell. He couldn't possibly pose any kind of threat.

Max slipped the belt out from the loops on his waistband, crouched down in front of the door and inserted the buckle spike into the lock. He maneuvered it around for a couple of minutes without any noticeable effect, then removed it and had a rethink. The spike was too straight. The tumblers of the lock were arranged in parallel. What he needed was a hook he could insert between the tumblers to push them back one after the other.

He slid the tip of the spike into the narrow gap between the door and the jamb and exerted pressure on it, hoping that the metal wouldn't snap. Slowly, the end bent at a right angle. That was better. Max put the modified implement back into the keyhole and probed the moving parts of the mechanism. *Click!* The first tumbler sprang back. Max peered into the keyhole.

How many tumblers were there? On complex locks there could be five or more. But on this old one there were probably three at the most. *Click!* The second tumbler snapped back. Max twisted the spike to get farther in and felt the tip break. He mouthed an expletive. That was the last thing he needed.

Pulling out the spike, he examined the end. The tip had sheared off, leaving a jagged point behind. There was still a slight hook, though. That might just be enough. Max put the spike back into the keyhole, pushing it in as far as he could. He twisted it and eventually felt it catch on something—the edge of the third tumbler. But the lock had rusted with age. The parts no longer moved as smoothly as they once had. Max increased the pressure. "Come on," he whispered. "Just a little bit farther."

It wasn't going to go: The lock was too stiff. Max squeezed the tip of his forefinger into the keyhole to get extra leverage and pushed on the spike. He felt the tumbler give a little. He kept pushing. The tumbler gave a bit more, then . . . it clicked back and the bolt disengaged.

Max stood up and grasped the door handle. This was a first for him—breaking out of a police cell—but it gave him no feeling of elation. He was too worried about Consuela. He depressed the handle. The steel door swung open. Max looked about cautiously. The cell block appeared to be deserted. He stepped out and edged slowly along to the end of the corridor. A flight of stairs went up to his left; on the right was a door that, he guessed, gave access to the backyard. He eased the door open a fraction. Yes, there was the yard, a black-and-white police car parked nearby against the wall.

The stairs were out of the question. Going up them into the heart of the police station would lead to certain capture. So the yard it was. But how could he get across without being spotted? The area was brightly lit, and there was a high metal gate topped with spikes across the exit, an intercom next to it that you presumably had to speak into to get it opened. Not good.

Voices rang out on the stairs. Max heard the heavy tread of boots. Someone was coming. He looked around in a panic. Where should he go? Back to his cell? No way. He'd only just got out of there. He pulled back the door and darted out. What now? The yard was bordered on three sides by buildings. Max couldn't see anywhere to hide. He'd just have to run for it, try to climb over the gate.

Then he had another idea. A reckless, totally wild idea that might just work. He ran over to the police patrol car, pulled open the rear door, and threw himself inside, turning round to close the door quietly behind him. He lay on the floor behind the front seats in the darkness, his heart pounding.

Those footsteps he'd heard, were they officers coming to see him in his cell? If they were, he was done for. They'd raise the alarm when they found him gone. Every nook and cranny of the police station and the yard would be searched until Max was located. But maybe they weren't coming to see him. Hopefully it would be morning before his escape was discovered.

He heard the voices again—two men speaking in Spanish as they crossed the yard. One of them laughed. They sounded relaxed, not like men who'd just found a cell door unlocked and a prisoner missing. The front doors of the police car opened. Max's heart missed a beat. The men were getting in.

The front seats rocked as the two police officers sank into them. Max held his breath, his body rigid. If the officers looked back . . .

The engine turned over. The two policemen kept talking. One of them lit a cigarette. The car moved off.

Max let the air out of his lungs and started breathing normally again. The sounds of the engine and the men's voices were loud enough to cover any slight noise he made.

At the exit barrier, the car paused. The driver spoke into the intercom and the gate swung open. The patrol car turned out into the street and accelerated.

For the next half hour they drove around the streets of Rio Verde, the men talking and smoking, Max lying motionless on the floor in the back. Then the radio crackled. A voice relayed a message in Spanish. Max listened intently for a mention of his name, but he didn't hear one. The officer in the passenger seat picked up the radio mike and acknowledged the message, then flipped a switch, turning on the patrol-car siren and roof light. The vehicle did a sharp U-turn and sped back the way it had come. For a moment, Max wondered whether they were returning to the police station, but then the patrol car careered round a corner and skidded to a halt. The officers jumped out. There were yells, the sound of glass breaking. Max lifted his head and risked a look out of the car window.

They were outside a bar in the center of the city. Four or five drunken young men brandishing beer bottles were brawling on the pavement. The police officers were busy breaking them apart.

Max moved fast. He opened the door on the road

side and slithered out on his belly. Getting to his feet, he looked round. The policemen were concentrating on breaking up the fight, the boys on getting away from the vicious baton blows. No one was looking Max's way. He dashed across the road and away down a side street.

The courtyard was in darkness, not a light burning in any of the windows. Max made his way carefully up the stairs to the third floor and knocked on an apartment door. When he got no response, he knocked again.

Bare feet padded on the tiles inside the apartment and a bolt slid back. The door opened a few inches on a chain and Isabella's wary eyes peered out. She recognized Max immediately. "It's you," she said softly in English. "What you want?"

"I need help," Max said.

"Is the middle of the night."

"Please, let me in. I have nowhere else to go."

"What you mean?"

"The police may be looking for me."

Isabella's eyes opened wide with fear. "The police? You must go away. I'm sorry, we no want any trouble."

She started to close the door, but Max jammed his foot in the gap to stop her.

"Please, listen to me," he said urgently. "Your dad

helped my dad. I need your help now. You can't turn me away."

"Is too dangerous."

Isabella pushed hard on the door, trying to force Max's foot out.

"Don't you want to know why your father was murdered?"

Isabella froze. She stared at Max. "What you say?"

"Let me in—we need to talk."

"Murdered?"

"Let me in, Isabella. This is important."

She hesitated for a second. Then she unhooked the chain and pulled back the door to let him in.

"My mother, she is at work. My brothers and sisters, they asleep. We must talk quietly. Come in here."

She led him into the kitchen and closed the door. She didn't turn on the light.

"What you know about my father?" she said.

Max sat down on a chair. He suddenly felt tired. The stress of being locked up, of escaping from the police station, was taking its toll.

"I know your father took my dad out in his boat. And I have a feeling they went to Isla de Sombra."

"No one goes there," Isabella said. "Is not allowed. I tell you that yesterday."

"Where else did they go? My dad didn't fish; he

didn't like the sea. He had to have a reason for hiring your dad and his boat—and there's something odd about that island, something sinister."

"Sinister? What that mean?"

"Evil."

"And my father? Why you say he was murdered?"

It was dark in the kitchen, but enough moonlight was filtering in through the window for Max to see how tense Isabella's face was. "I don't know it for certain," he said gently. "But it's suspicious, isn't it? Your father takes my dad out in his boat. A couple of days later my dad disappears. Everyone thinks he's dead. Then shortly afterward *your* dad dies."

"He fall into sea and drown," Isabella said.

"How could that have happened? He was an experienced sailor."

"The sea, it is rough. Fishermen drown—it happen a lot."

"But the timing's suspicious. It's too much of a coincidence."

Isabella's hair was loose around her shoulders. She scooped it away from her face and looked hard at Max. "Who would kill him? Why?"

"I don't know," Max answered. "But I think that island is the key."

He told her what had happened. About Consuela

disappearing from the hotel, his arrest, his escape from custody. Everything.

"You escape from police?" Isabella said in alarm. "They will come here. The police here in Santo Domingo, they are not good men."

"I'll go soon," Max said. He couldn't put Isabella and her family at risk. Maybe he shouldn't have come there. "That ruined building you took me to yesterday—is it a safe place?"

"For a few hours, yes."

"I'll hole up there."

"Then what you do?"

"I think they've taken Consuela to Shadow Island," Max said. "What more do you know about that place?"

"I never been there. All I know is what I already tell you. Señor Clark, he own it. Before him, government own it. It was prison. And long time ago it was pirate fortress."

"Do you have a map of it?"

"No map. I never see map of the island."

"Or any books? Are there any books about it that I could look at? Anything that might show the layout of the fortress?"

"You want to know where rooms are?"

"Yes, that kind of thing."

Isabella was silent for a time. Max could see she was

frowning, thinking about what he'd told her.

"You can trust me, Isabella," he said reassuringly. "If I find out what really happened to my father, maybe I'll find out what really happened to yours, too."

"There is man," Isabella said. "Angel Romero. He was friend of my father's. He has been to Isla de Sombra."

"He has? When?"

"Years ago. When it was prison."

"He was a prisoner there? Could I talk to him?"

"He is old now, sick."

"Does he live in Rio Verde?"

"Yes, with his daughter."

"Can I meet him?"

Isabella didn't reply immediately. Max didn't push her. She knew almost nothing about him. He'd come there in the middle of the night, asking her for help, perhaps putting her and her family in danger.

"Okay," she said finally. "In the morning I come and find you. I take you to him."

13

RUPERT PENHALL GAZED ACROSS THE DESK at Colonel Pablo de los Mantequillas. His face was expressionless, but the chief of police was clearly a very angry man. Beneath the suntan, his cheeks were hot and flushed and his eyes burned with fury. If there was one thing he hated, it was being made to look a fool.

"The oafs! The incompetent, stupid, lazy oafs!" he exclaimed vehemently. "I'll have every last one of them lined up in the yard, where I'll take great pleasure in giving their backsides a good kicking."

"How did it happen?" Penhall asked.

"I don't know. No one knows," Colonel Mantequillas

replied. "Someone went down to his cell at six o'clock this morning and found the door unlocked and the boy gone."

"Do you know when he escaped?"

"No. It could have been anytime during the night. My men had strict instructions to check him at regular intervals, but they were all too idle to bother. They'll pay for that; I'll make sure of it."

"I advised you not to underestimate him, Colonel."

"He was handcuffed and locked in a cell. Someone must have helped him. He can't have done all this by himself. He's just a boy. What is he—thirteen, fourteen years old?"

"He's fourteen."

"He must have bribed one of my men. I'm having them all questioned, and when I find out who it was, I'll—"

"He didn't have help," Penhall broke in.

Mantequillas eyed him narrowly. "No? What makes you so sure?"

"He's an escape artist—like his father. That's what he does. He gets out of handcuffs, picks locks. How did he get out of the police station?"

The chief looked away, embarrassed by the question. "We believe he may have hidden in the back of a police car that was going out on patrol," he admitted.

"You mean, your men actually *drove* him away from the station?" Penhall said incredulously.

"It would appear so."

"And the officers didn't notice?"

"They have both been suspended without pay. Far greater punishment will follow, you can take my word for that."

"You are looking for him?"

"Of course we're looking for him," Mantequillas snapped. He disliked being questioned by this arrogant Englishman. "We are searching the entire city. I have men watching the bus station, the airport, the river. He won't get far."

"What about the Gonzales house?"

"We have checked it. He isn't there."

"I know where he'll try to go," Penhall said. "To the island."

Mantequillas looked skeptical. "You think so? What does he know about it?"

"Nothing much, I'm sure. But he's a clever kid. He can work things out."

"Then I'll put more men on watch by the harbor," the police chief said. "We'll catch him."

"No, don't do that."

"What?"

"Let him play into our hands. Let him go out there. But tell the guards to expect him."

"And then what?"

Penhall shrugged. "There's no way he will escape from there alive."

Max spent a cold, uncomfortable night huddled in the ruined building down the street from Isabella's apartment. He didn't sleep much. It was too chilly and he had too much on his mind.

At daybreak, he heard someone scrambling over the rubble, a voice whispering his name. He stood up. "Over here."

It was Isabella. She'd brought him a piece of bread and a bottle of water. Max realized he'd eaten nothing since lunchtime the previous day. He wolfed down the bread and took a long gulp of water.

"The police, they came," Isabella said.

Max swallowed. His stomach lurched. He lowered the bottle and gazed at her. She looked pale and strained. "When?"

"An hour ago. They search the apartment, ask us questions about you. They know you come to the apartment yesterday afternoon. But not during the night."

"What did you tell them?"

"Some truth, some lies. I say you come, yes, ask about your father and the boat trip. I say nothing about Isla de Sombra."

Max looked over her shoulder, scanning the entrance to the ruined building. "What if they're watching your apartment?"

"I am careful. I look. There is no one. Come, I take you to Angel Romero now."

They didn't go back out onto the street. They went through a hole in the wall on the far side of the building, slithered down a dirt bank, then crossed a yard, emerging in an alley lower down the hill.

It was a ten-minute walk to Angel Romero's house— a small, single-story wooden shack tucked away in a gloomy courtyard behind what looked like a warehouse. Max waited outside while Isabella went in to talk to Romero.

"He will see us," she said when she returned. "But he is not well. We cannot stay long."

Angel Romero was a hunched, frail-looking man with thinning gray hair and a lined face. Isabella had told Max he was only in his late fifties, but he appeared at least twenty years older. Judging by his bone structure, he must once have been a strong man, but now the flesh had fallen away from him and he was stooped and shrunken. He was sitting in an armchair in the corner of his kitchen, drinking coffee. When he lifted his mug, his hand shook so much that the coffee spilled over the rim and trickled down onto his knees. His daughter, Victoria, immediately stepped forward with a dishcloth and dabbed at his trousers to dry them off. Romero waved her away impatiently. "Don't fuss, child, I'm all right," he said in Spanish.

Then he turned to Max and spoke in fluent English. "Sit down. So you want to know about Isla de Sombra."

Max sat on a stool. Romero's gaze was shrewd and direct. His body might have deteriorated, but his mind was still sharp.

"Isabella told me you were once a prisoner there," Max said.

"Yes, I was. A long time ago. Do you know anything about the history of our country?"

"Only a bit," Max said. "I read some stuff on the internet before I came out here."

"You know about Juan Cruz, the Partido Democrático Popular leader?"

"Juan Cruz? He was the president who was assassinated, wasn't he?"

"Gunned down outside his house by paramilitary thugs working for the generals who'd been in power before Cruz. I was one of his supporters, as were millions of other people in this country. Juan Cruz was a fine man, a man who believed in justice and equality. He wanted to remove the gap between rich and poor so that everyone would have clean water, enough to eat, schools and health care for their children. When he died, that dream died with him."

"The generals took power again after he was assassinated, didn't they?" Max said.

"And they've been in power ever since," Romero replied. "And look what our country is like now. Have you seen much of it?"

"A bit of Rio Verde and Playa d'Oro, that's all."

"You've been to Playa d'Oro? That sums it up perfectly. On the one hand you have peasant farmers and workers who can barely earn enough to feed their families. On the other you have Playa d'Oro, that playground for the rich and idle where no one does anything except sunbathe, gamble, and eat. In Rio Verde, there are power cuts every night. You know why? Because Playa d'Oro takes all the electricity to light the casino and the restaurants. In Rio Verde there is no water after nine P.M. Playa d'Oro takes it all. Not for people to drink, but to water the golf course and fill the swimming pools. That is what the generals have done for Santo Domingo." Romero broke off in a fit of coughing.

Victoria came forward again, a concerned expression on her face. "Papa, you shouldn't talk so much. It's not good for you," she said in Spanish.

Romero took a sip of coffee. "I am fine," he said hoarsely. "Leave me alone."

He looked back at Max, speaking in English again. "My chest is not good. I have Shadow Island to thank for that. The conditions in which we were kept there destroyed my health."

"Why were you sent to that place?" Max asked.

"Because I opposed the generals. I was a member of the PDP. After Cruz was killed, there were demonstrations all over the country. The people took to the streets to protest, and the generals used that as an excuse to send in the army. Dozens of peaceful protesters were shot. Others—like me—were rounded up and imprisoned without trial. The ones the generals regarded as the biggest threat were executed. I was only a small fish, a teacher of English in a secondary school, so I was sent to Shadow Island."

"For how long?"

"I was there for eight years. It is a terrible place. The memories still give me nightmares. Why would you, a young boy from England, be interested in it?"

Max told him about his father, and about Consuela being taken by the police. "I think she may be on the island. If I wanted to go there, how would I do it?"

"You can't. It is not possible," Romero said.

"There *must* be a way. Do you remember much about the fortress?"

"I remember everything. There are some things in life you never forget. Shadow Island is one of those things."

Max turned to Isabella, who was sitting on a bench with Romero's daughter, listening intently to every word of their conversation. She passed him a pad of paper and a pen she'd brought with her.

"Could you draw a plan of the fortress for me?" Max asked Romero.

"You shouldn't think about even attempting to go there," Romero said. "You will never get into the fortress. And you could be killed trying."

"Consuela is there. I'm not going to leave her," Max said staunchly.

Romero studied Max's face, seeing the steely determination in his eyes.

"Give me the paper." Romero took the pad and pen and began to draw, describing the layout of the fortress as the pen moved across the paper. "It's on several floors," he said. "The heart of the fortress dates back to the sixteenth century, when pirates built a stone tower on the top of the cliffs to keep watch for Spanish ships carrying gold coming north from Panama. There are rumored to be caves and tunnels beneath the fortress that the pirates dug in case they ever had to escape from the island, but I never saw any sign of them."

Romero paused again as another bout of coughing racked his body. He doubled over, his shoulders and chest heaving.

Max watched anxiously. "I'm sorry," he said. "I'm asking too much of you." He looked at Victoria. "Should we go?"

It was Romero who answered. "No, stay. I will be all right. Just give me a moment."

His breath was coming in loud wheezes and his face was flushed. He drank some more of his coffee and cleared his throat. A minute passed before he found the strength to continue speaking. "After the pirates had been driven from the waters off Santo Domingo, the Spanish turned Shadow Island into a naval fortress and added most of the buildings that are still there today."

Romero drew a square surrounded by smaller squares and rectangles. The pen lines were fuzzy and uneven because his hand was so unsteady. "There is a central courtyard here, and round it are different rooms. When I was there, this area on the north side was the guards' quarters and the governor's office. These rooms on the west and south were the kitchens and dining area. I don't know what they're used for now."

"And you?" Max said. "Where were you and the other prisoners kept?"

"All over. There were cells up here on the third and fourth floors, and more down in the dungeons. They were the worst. They were infested with rats and had no windows, so the prisoners lived in permanent darkness. When they eventually came out, some after many years, the sunlight blinded them. Literally burned out their eyes, they were so unused to it."

Romero added some more lines to his sketch. "These are the staircases. One in each wing. And this is the main door. It was made of wood studded with iron rivets and was guarded day and night by armed soldiers."

"Did anyone ever escape?" Max asked.

"A few tried, but none succeeded. Some jumped off the battlements into the sea and tried to swim for it, but the currents around the island are very strong, very dangerous. Not one survived. Another man tried to get through an old sewage outlet—a long pipe leading underground from the toilets to the sea. But the pipe was narrow and full of water. The man drowned. The guards dragged out his body and left it hanging in the courtyard for a week, as a warning to the rest of us of what would happen if we tried to escape."

"This pipe—show me where it was on your plan."

"Here, on the southeast corner. You're not thinking of trying to get in that way, are you?"

"I don't know what I'm thinking," Max said.

"It would be suicide. The pipe is a hundred yards long. It is full of water and too narrow for scuba equipment. No one could get through it."

Romero held out the pad of paper. "I admire your concern for your friend," he said. "But if she is on Shadow Island, you will not be able to get to her. The island is heavily guarded. No one knows what they do there now. Scientific research, some people say, but I do not know if that is true. Julius Clark, the island owner, can do whatever he likes. He has powerful friends in the Santo Domingan government. In America, too."

"And Britain?"

"Yes, Britain. He controls many businesses. He is like an octopus. His tentacles are everywhere. If you cross him, he will throttle you."

Max took the pad. It was only then that he noticed Romero's left hand. One of the fingers was missing. Max stared at the scarred stump.

"What's the matter?" Romero asked.

"Your hand . . . ," Max stammered. "It's . . ."

"I know, it's not a pretty sight," Romero said. "Another legacy of Shadow Island. There were beatings and other punishments for minor breaches of prison rules, but if you did something really serious, the guards would take an axe and chop off one of your fingers, sometimes more than one."

"I met a man from Santo Domingo in London," Max said. "He had two missing fingers. His name was Luis Lopez-Vega."

Romero stared at him in astonishment. "*Luis?* You met Luis? When was this?"

"Last week."

"*Last week?* Surely not."

"Do you know him?" Max said.

"Of course. Luis was a prisoner on Shadow Island at the same time as I was. What was he doing in London?"

"He was murdered before I could find out."

"*Murdered?* My God, what happened?"

"He was shot in his hotel room."

Romero looked away. "That is sad news," he said. "Luis was a good man."

"The London police are saying he was a drug dealer. That he had been in prison for drug-related offenses."

Romero gave a contemptuous snort. "The London police know nothing about Santo Domingo, about how things work here. Yes, Luis was in prison recently. But he wasn't a drug dealer. The charges were fabricated. The police do that to people they want to get out of the way. Luis was jailed because he was a political activist. He was one of the core group of fighters who opposed the generals in the seventies, who kept the PDP going underground when the government banned it. He was a threat to the generals, so they locked him away. I heard that he'd been released, but I did not know he was dead."

"He told me that my father was alive," Max said. "But he died before he could explain. You don't know anything about that, do you?"

Romero shook his head. "I lost contact with Luis and his friends a long time ago. I am too sick to do anything more for the PDP. I cannot do even light work. I am dependent on my daughter to support me." He glanced tenderly at Victoria. "Without her, I would not survive."

Victoria went over and placed her hand on his shoulder. "You should rest now, Papa." She turned to Max and Isabella. "I'm sorry, but please, you must go. My father is tired."

Max nodded and stood up. "Thank you for your help," he said to Romero. "Can I ask one last question? Do the numbers one-one-one-three-eight-three-five-two mean anything to you?"

"No," Romero said after a moment. "They mean nothing."

Victoria showed Max and Isabella out of the house and they walked up the street, Max studying the drawings Romero had made on the pad of paper.

"What are you going to do now?" Isabella asked.

Max thought for a moment. "When we talked yesterday, you said you still had your father's boat. Is it seaworthy?"

"Seaworthy? What you mean?"

"Is it okay to use?"

"Yes, is okay."

"And can you sail it?"

"Yes. I go out with my father many times. I know what to do. Why you ask?"

"I want you to take me to Isla de Sombra," Max said.

14

MAX CLAMBERED ONTO A NARROW RIDGE of rocks and watched the fishing boat come round the headland from Rio Verde. He could see Isabella in the boat's wheelhouse. She raised her hand, letting him know she'd spotted him, and changed course, heading toward the shore.

Max hadn't dared go down to the harbor with her. He knew the police would be keeping an eye out for him, searching the streets of the capital, paying particular attention to the exit points—the roads, the river, and the sea.

It wasn't safe for Max to go anywhere near Fernando Gonzales's fishing boat, but no one would be suspicious if Gonzales's daughter took it out. Max had given Isabella some of his Santo Domingan currency to buy fuel—he could see from their tiny, cramped apartment that they didn't have much money. He then walked two miles out of the capital along back streets and rough dirt tracks to their rendezvous on the coast.

The boat slowed and came to a virtual stop fifty yards out, Isabella giving the throttle occasional short bursts of power to hold her position. She couldn't get any closer for fear of being swept onto the rocks by the rolling waves.

Max slid into the water and swam out to the boat, hauling himself up a knotted rope to the stern deck. Dripping wet, he went to join Isabella in the wheelhouse. "Any problems?" he said.

Isabella shook her head, her ponytail swinging across her shoulders. "No. The harbormaster, the other fishermen, they all know me."

"Did they ask where you were going?"

"I say I just go along coast short distance. To keep boat engine working. Leave boat in harbor too long, it no good for engine."

Max smiled at her. "Thank you for helping me. I know you're taking a big risk."

"I want to find out what happen to my father."

Isabella thrust the throttle forward and the boat surged away. It was a short, stubby little vessel with a sun-bleached hull and the name *Rosario* painted on the side of the wheelhouse.

"Is my mother's name," Isabella had told him earlier, describing the *Rosario* so that Max knew which boat to look out for when he was waiting on the rocks.

Isabella swung the wheel over to port and they headed out to sea.

"How close can you get to the island?" Max asked.

"Not very. I told you, there is boat. Men come out, tell you to go away. But I try to get near."

Max crouched low so he wasn't visible to anyone watching them from Shadow Island—and he was pretty sure someone *would* be watching. If Julius Clark valued his privacy enough to have a patrol boat keeping unwanted visitors away, then he'd almost certainly have a lookout who'd spot any vessel that threatened to stray too close.

It was a still day, but even so the *Rosario* rolled a lot in the swell. She seemed a sturdy enough boat, but Max wouldn't have wanted to be out in her in a storm. He peered through the side window of the wheelhouse. Shadow Island was a couple of miles away

201

to the north, still too far for him to be able to make out any of the details.

"Can we get nearer?" he said.

Isabella adjusted their course. "There are binoculars in there," she said, nodding at a locker on the floor.

Max lifted the lid and saw life jackets, a tarpaulin, an emergency flare, and various ropes inside. He rummaged underneath the life jackets and found a scuffed leather case containing a pair of ancient binoculars.

He trained the binoculars on Shadow Island and adjusted the focus. He could see the rocks at the base of the island, the sheer cliffs above them with the stone fortress on top.

"Are there rocks all the way round?" Max asked.

"Yes."

"So how do you land on it?"

"There is jetty. That is only place," Isabella said. "On southwest corner. You see it?"

"Yes, I see."

The jetty was made of huge blocks of stone like the ones that had been used to build the fortress. It protruded about twenty or thirty yards from the island, coming out beyond the rocks to provide deepwater mooring for boats. Max could see a vessel there now—a sleek, streamlined launch with a small forest of radio antennae and satellite-navigation equipment on its cabin roof. It looked very expensive and very fast. Not the kind of vessel that you could outrun in a battered old tub like the *Rosario*.

Max studied the island. He had never seen such an impregnable-looking place. There was an uninterrupted rim of sharp rocks that made approaching by boat hazardous. Then, even if you got over that obstacle, there was a sheer sixty-foot-high cliff in front of you that only an expert mountaineer with ropes and pitons would be able to scale. Above the cliffs were the smooth, high stone walls of the fortress, which no one, not even a skillful climber, would be able to tackle. Max could see why marauding buccaneers had once made it their base.

"Do you think you can get close to the southeast corner?" he said.

Isabella looked at him, her expression concerned. "You think about that pipe? Angel Romero said you die if you try to swim it."

"It could be my only way onto the island," Max replied. "I'm a good underwater swimmer. I want to see what it looks like."

"It very dangerous. This Consuela, she must be very special."

"She is."

Isabella studied him a moment, then turned the wheel and opened the throttle a little. The *Rosario* headed across the sea toward the island. Max waited until they were a hundred yards off the southeast corner, then stripped down to his boxer shorts. Isabella adjusted the engine and rudder until the boat was side on to the island.

"Okay," she said. "This as close as I can get."

Max went down on all fours and crawled across the deck before slipping over the starboard side, knowing that the bulk of the wheelhouse had shielded his actions from any watching eyes on Shadow Island.

He swam under the hull of the boat and kept going underwater toward the island. The water was clear, but too deep for him to see the bottom.

After fifty yards the rock shelf loomed up ahead of him and he felt the tide pulling on his body. The waves on the surface were beginning to break over the rocks, so he swam deeper to keep out of the turbulence.

Max scanned the edge of the rock shelf where it plunged down in what appeared to be a bottomless subterranean cliff. The shelf was composed of layers of jagged rock, the uneven edges softened by a thick coat of seaweed. Where was the pipe? It had to be somewhere around here. Max swam closer. How long had he been underwater? A minute? Maybe a minute and a half. He was still feeling comfortable, but knew he'd have to surface for air pretty soon.

The shelf was close enough to touch now. Max stretched out a hand and ran his fingers over the carpet of seaweed. Was he in the right place? He'd thought the opening of the pipe would be obvious, but he couldn't see it. He turned and swam along parallel to the shelf, examining the rocks as he went. Maybe the pipe wasn't there any longer. Maybe Romero had remembered its position incorrectly.

Max felt a pain in his chest: His body was running out of oxygen. He kicked upward. As he broke the surface, he snatched a mouthful of air but saw a big wave rolling toward him. He ducked back down quickly before he was swept onto the rocks. He hadn't filled his lungs. He needed more air if he was to stay under for any further length of time. He went back up to the surface. This time there was a gap between waves. He took a huge gulp of air and dived back down to resume his search.

Twice more he had to surface for air. He was becoming demoralized. Where *was* this pipe? He had to find it. Isabella could only stay nearby for a limited period of time. If the patrol boat came out and ordered her to move away, Max would be stranded, with no means of getting back to the shore. Romero had said the currents off the island were treacherous. Max was a strong swimmer, but he didn't rate his chances of making it back to the mainland through an angry ocean.

Perhaps he'd missed the opening of the pipe. He turned and swam back the way he'd come. With breaks for air, he must have been underwater for seven or eight minutes. He was getting tired. He peered at the rocks but could still see nothing resembling a pipe. There were clefts and hollows and deep crevasses and—

Max stopped abruptly and swam back a couple of yards. He'd noticed a distinct shape in the layer of seaweed—a long, rounded ridge running back toward the island. He put his hand on the seaweed but could feel nothing solid beneath. He pushed his fingers deeper. It was hollow behind the seaweed. Max ripped away some of the trailing fronds and saw a dark, circular opening—he'd found the pipe.

Using both hands now, he tore off the rest of the

seaweed curtain and gazed into the hole beyond. It was about two feet in diameter, but it was too dark to see very far. Max put his head and shoulders in. The pipe was wide enough for him to swim through, but was it clear all the way to the end? And how long was it? A hundred yards, Romero had said. But was he right?

Max felt himself running out of air. He propelled himself up to the surface and trod water for a time, filling his aching lungs. He looked across toward the jetty, and his blood went cold. The patrol boat was racing out toward them.

Max took a deep breath and dived back under the water. He didn't think anyone on the patrol boat had seen him—it was too far away for that—but he had to get back to the *Rosario* before the patrol boat reached it. It was less than a hundred yards. He could do that distance easily without coming up for air. But could he do it fast enough? He kicked hard, pushing himself to the limit. He'd never swum so fast in his life. He saw the hull of the *Rosario* in front of him and glanced back. He couldn't see the patrol boat yet. He just needed a few more seconds, that was all. The *Rosario* was almost over him now. Isabella would be able to see him in the clear water. Max swam underneath the boat, surfacing on the starboard side. He clung to the trailing bow rope, gasping for air.

The patrol boat approached, coming to a stop a few yards away from the *Rosario*. A soldier with a submachine gun in his arms called out to Isabella in Spanish.

"These are private waters. What are you doing here?"

"I've come to fish," Isabella shouted back.

"Fishing is forbidden. You should know that. Move away now."

"What?"

"Move away."

The soldier let off an angry burst of submachine gunfire, peppering the water between the two boats. "Next time, we'll sink you."

Isabella scurried into the wheelhouse and rammed the throttle forward. The *Rosario* sped away, Max hidden from the soldier's view. He clung tightly to the bow rope and was towed along, the water buffeting his body. Only when they were well away from the patrol boat did Isabella throttle back and stop. Max hauled himself up onto the deck and crawled into the wheelhouse.

Isabella was ashen-faced. The gunfire had terri-fied her. "Thank God you are safe!" she exclaimed, exhaling with relief. "I see you come under boat, but after that I don't know what happen to you."

"I'm okay," Max said, still a little breathless after his battering in the water. "You're not hurt?"

"Not hurt. Just scared. We should not stay here longer."

Max looked back at the island. He picked up the binoculars and trained them on the jetty, half a mile away. Two men came down the steep steps from the fortress and walked out along it. They were dressed in military fatigues and carried submachine guns over their shoulders.

"Look!" Isabella said.

She was pointing diagonally ahead: A motor launch identical to the one that had left the jetty was speeding toward the island from the south.

Max watched the launch through the binoculars. It slowed and came alongside the jetty. Two sailors leaped ashore and tied the boat to a couple of mooring posts. Then a short gangplank was extended and a man was escorted off. He wore a blue shirt and faded jeans. Max couldn't see his face. He was walking a little unsteadily, his arms in a strange position. Max realized with a jolt of shock that he was handcuffed.

The two armed guards took hold of the man and

led him away along the jetty. They went slowly up the steps and through the big iron-studded wooden doors at the main entrance to the fortress.

Max lowered his binoculars. "You're right, we should go," he said.

Isabella pushed the throttle lever forward. "Did you find the pipe?"

Max nodded.

"Can you swim it?"

"I don't know. We'll find out tonight."

15

IT WAS A MOONLESS NIGHT, THE SKY SO
overcast that not a single star shone through the canopy
of cloud. The *Rosario* was almost invisible on the black
expanse of the ocean. Isabella kept the wheelhouse and
navigation lights off, steering in complete darkness.
Max was standing beside her. He'd spent the afternoon
and evening hiding in a cave on the shore, waiting for
night to fall and Isabella to return. He'd swum out to
the boat from the headland once again, and his clothes
were dripping wet. There was a towel in the wheelhouse, but Max didn't bother to dry even his hair. He
was going to be wet again all too soon.

There was a wind blowing offshore, breaking the

surface of the sea. The waves were higher than they'd been earlier in the day, and the *Rosario* was pitching and tossing, spray showering over the deck.

Isabella couldn't see the compass or any other navigation aid, but she didn't need to. Their destination was clearly visible on the horizon, lights burning in the windows of the fortress and down by the jetty.

"You sure you want to do this?" she said.

"I'm sure."

"I'll get as close as I can. How long do I give you?"

"Twenty minutes. If I'm not back in that time, you can assume I'm inside the fortress."

Isabella glanced at him. Neither of them made any mention of the alternative outcome: After twenty minutes, Max might not be inside the fortress, but dead.

"We can still go back," Isabella said. "Forget this plan."

"No, I'm going ahead with it," Max answered firmly.

"It very dangerous. Maybe very foolish. Is there really no other way of getting onto the island?"

"We wouldn't even get close to the jetty; it's too well protected. Those trigger-happy guards would probably shoot us if we went too near. And the cliffs are unclimbable, you can see that. The pipe is the only way. I *have* to get to Consuela."

Isabella didn't argue further. She pulled back the throttle lever. The boat slowed. "This is where we were this morning," she said.

Max picked up the waterproof flashlight Isabella had bought earlier in Rio Verde and stuffed it down the waistband of his trousers. "I'll see you," he said.

"Good luck," Isabella replied.

Max dropped over the side of the boat and started to swim toward Shadow Island. He stayed on the surface, to see where he was going and to conserve his lung power, but the rough sea didn't make it easy. The waves kept rolling over him, breaking in his face. He had to judge his position exactly. If he got too close to the island before he submerged, he risked being dashed on the rocks.

He looked up at the fortress, now less than a hundred yards away. He tried to gauge the exact location of the sewage outlet, but in the darkness he couldn't find his bearings. Everything looked different at night. He'd just have to dive down and search for it again. He ducked beneath the surface and swam to the edge of the rock shelf.

Pulling the flashlight from his waistband, he clicked it on and shone the beam over the rocks. A fish darted away in front of him, surprised by the light. The sea-weed glowed a dozen different shades of green, fronds and tendrils swaying in the underwater currents.

There it was—the opening to the sewage outlet. Max shone the flashlight inside the pipe. It lit up the first few yards, but after that there was just a black hole.

Max swam to the surface again and trod water, breathing in deeply, preparing himself for the challenge he was about to undertake. The idea of swimming through that dark, narrow pipe filled him with dread. He didn't suffer from claustrophobia. Small enclosed spaces didn't worry him, nor did water. Not as a general rule, anyway. He was used to being shut up in boxes and trunks and immersed in water. But he'd never attempted anything like this. He didn't know what was inside the pipe, and he'd get only one chance to find out. If fate was against him, this seaweed-encrusted outlet might very easily become his tomb.

Max turned his head. The *Rosario* was now just a small shadow bobbing up and down on the sea. He didn't know whether Isabella would be able to see him—probably not—but he raised his arm and waved to her just in case. Then he braced himself. He couldn't put off the moment any longer. Delaying only encouraged him to dwell on the hazards of what he was about to do. As Isabella had said, this was a dangerous venture, a foolish one. But he knew he had no choice. Consuela was on Shadow Island, and he knew in his gut that the island was in some way connected to his father's disappearance.

He took a deep breath, filling every tiny recess of his lungs with air, and dived down once more. He placed his right hand on the edge of the outlet for a second, to steady himself, then plunged inside the pipe. The walls closed around him. They were made of iron, the surfaces pitted and eaten away by rust. Every couple of yards there was a riveted sleeve where the cylindrical sections had been joined together.

The flashlight beam pierced the blackness, but Max could see no end to the pipe. The water was cloudy. He could feel the pressure on his body, on his eardrums. How far had he come? Twenty, thirty yards? That was only a quarter of the distance he had to cover. He'd been underwater for less than a minute. He had about two more minutes of air in his lungs, but was that going to be enough? He couldn't turn back—the pipe was too narrow for that. A chill passed through him. What if the other end of the pipe was blocked? What if he found there was no way out after all? He would die down here.

He resisted the temptation to increase his speed. That would use up his remaining oxygen too fast. *Just keep going at an even pace*, he told himself. *Stay calm. Don't think about anything other than the next stroke. One yard at a time.* He let some air trickle out through his lips to relieve the pressure on his lungs. His eardrums were in agony. It felt as if a sharp nail were jabbing into them.

His legs and arms kept up a steady rhythm, propelling him along the cylinder. It seemed to Max that the pipe was getting narrower, but he wondered if it was just his imagination.

How far had he come now? Sixty yards? Seventy? He still couldn't see the end, and he was running out of air. It felt as if there was a hoop of steel around his chest getting tighter and tighter. He let out some more air, watching the bubbles float up past his eyes.

Was it another trick of his imagination, or had the pipe started to slope upward a little? Yes, he could definitely feel a slight change. But the end was still nowhere in sight. He must have swum ninety yards by now. Surely he must be close to the fortress. His lungs were bursting. He couldn't hold his breath for much longer.

Then the flashlight beam struck something in the

blackness ahead. Max saw rivets, a wall of rusty iron, and his heart almost stopped. The pipe was blocked. He'd reached a dead end. His fingers touched the wall, probing the surface, pushing hard on it. It was solid metal. That was it. He'd come all this way for nothing. He had only a few seconds of air left. Should he try to turn around, make an attempt to swim back out? Max knew it was futile, but he wasn't going to just wait there passively for the end. If he was going to die, he wanted to die doing something.

He twisted his body. One arm scraped against the side of the pipe. His other arm flailed upward . . . but it encountered no resistance. There was nothing there. Max rolled over onto his back and shone the flashlight directly up. The pipe hadn't come to an end. It had simply turned through a sharp ninety-degree angle.

Max thrust himself upward. His lungs were almost ready to explode. His vision was blurring; he was start-ing to feel dizzy. Another few seconds and he would black out. He scooped the water back frantically with his arms, his legs kicking out again and again. There was nothing left in his lungs. This was it. He felt him-self losing consciousness. He closed his eyes and kicked out one last time.

Then, suddenly, everything changed. There was no

longer water on his face, but cool air. He opened his eyes. He'd broken the surface. His head was out of the water. He gulped in the air greedily. The pain in his ears eased, the hoop around his chest relaxed.

He'd done it. He'd got through the pipe. And he was alive.

He could have whooped with delight, only he didn't have the energy. He trod water, shining the flashlight around. He was in a small stone-walled chamber that was partially flooded with seawater. At one side of the chamber, just above the water level, was a stone ledge with a rusty iron ladder bolted to the wall above. Max swam over to it and pulled himself out. He was exhausted. For three or four minutes he just lay on his back, breathing heavily.

He heard a slight movement by his feet and sat up, aiming the flashlight down. The beam reflected back off a pair of beady eyes—a rat. The creature gazed at Max, then scuttled away through a hole in the wall. Max dragged himself to his feet. His clothes were sodden and heavy with water. He stripped and wrung them out before dressing again. Then he grabbed hold of a rung and climbed up the rusty ladder.

There was an iron manhole cover at the top. Max clung to the highest rung with one hand and pushed on the cover with his other. It didn't move. He hammered on it with his fist. The cover still didn't budge. Max swung back off the ladder so he was almost upside down and slammed the sole of his sneaker into it. He felt it give a little. He kicked again, then swung back upright and pushed with his hand. The cover lifted out of its slot. Max pushed it to one side and clambered through the opening.

Shining the flashlight around, he saw that he was in the cellars of the fortress. There were stone slabs on the floor and a high vaulted ceiling above. The place smelled damp and musty. The beam of the flashlight found a door on the far side of the room. He walked over and tried the handle. The door was locked, but Max had come prepared. He rummaged in his trouser pockets, pulling out a small screwdriver and a piece of thick wire that he'd taken from the toolbox on board the *Rosario*. He shone the flashlight into the keyhole, assessing the lock, then chose the piece of wire as the best tool for the job. Ten seconds later, the lock slid back and Max inched open the door.

There was a corridor outside, with doors at regular intervals along both sides. Max had memorized the plan Angel Romero had drawn and knew that these doors gave access to the pitch-black, windowless cells in which political prisoners had been kept during the 1970s. *Are people still being kept in them?* Max wondered. Consuela was being held somewhere in the fortress—and what had happened to the handcuffed man who'd arrived that morning? Max didn't think either of them was down here in the cellars. From the stale, airless atmosphere, he got the impression that this area was no longer used. But he tried one of the doors anyway. It wasn't locked. Pushing it open, he heard the scurry of tiny paws inside and his flashlight caught the tails of half a dozen rats disappearing through a crack in the crumbling stonework.

The cell was one of the tiniest, most horrific rooms Max had ever seen. It was only about a five feet square—not even big enough for a man to lie down in. The floor was bare earth and the stone walls were damp and covered in a white, foul-smelling fungus. Max closed the door, imagining what it must have been like for the prisoners who'd been shut away in these ghastly cells, sometimes for years. How had they endured it?

Max walked on quickly to the staircase at the end of the corridor. He paused for a moment, then went cautiously up. As he neared the ground floor, he slowed, listening hard. The cellars might be out of use, but the rest of the fortress would certainly be occupied. He didn't want to blunder into one of the armed guards who he was sure patrolled the building. This floor didn't interest him. Romero had said the other cells were all on the third and fourth. If Consuela was locked away somewhere, it would probably be up there.

Max peered around the corner and saw a wide hallway with doors opening off it. The hall was in darkness, but through a window Max could see the courtyard in the center of the fortress, illuminated by floodlights. He crept across to the window and looked out warily. It appeared to be deserted at first, but then Max caught movement over by the main entrance: A figure stirred restlessly in the shadows. There was a guard on duty.

Max's plan of action was vague. It had consisted of two main objectives: getting into the fortress and rescuing Consuela. The first objective had been achieved; the second had still to be completed. Max hadn't given much thought to what happened after that. The important thing was finding Consuela. Once he'd done that, he'd worry about the minor details—like how they'd get out of the fortress and off the island without being recaptured or shot.

He pulled away from the window and ran lightly up the next flight of stairs. It was the middle of the night. With any luck, everyone would be asleep and he'd find

Consuela without encountering any opposition.

On the second-floor landing, Max paused again. He thought he'd heard something. Cocking his head, he listened. He *had* heard something. Someone was coming down the stairs. Max had to think fast. There was no point in going back to the ground floor, so that left him only one option. He ran along the landing and tried the handle of the first door he came to. It swung open a few inches. Max squinted through the gap, checking that the room was empty, then stepped inside and closed the door behind him. He waited, letting his eyes adjust to the darkness. He was in an office of some kind. There was a desk over by the window, cupboards on the walls. He could make out the details quite easily. Then he realized why. Light was seeping in under the door of an adjoining room.

Crouching down, Max looked through the keyhole of the door. He couldn't see much—just a wooden balustrade and a white wall beyond it. There was no sign of any people and no sound, either. Max eased open the door and went through. He found himself not in a room, as he'd expected, but on a gallery overlooking a very old, vast chamber. There was oak paneling on the walls, and the high ceiling was divided up into a series of painted squares separated by ornate plasterwork.

Max guessed it was probably the original main hall of the fortress, dating back to the sixteenth century.

But if the overall structure of the room was old, its contents were anything but. Max went to the balustrade and looked down. In the center of the hall below were two chairs—high-tech metal reclining ones like something out of a dentist's surgery. Arranged in a wide circle around them were various monitors, computers, and other pieces of machinery that Max couldn't identify. And at the edges of the room were stainless-steel benches and bits of apparatus that reminded him of the chemistry rooms at his school, only cleaner and newer. It was obviously some kind of scientific research laboratory.

He heard a door open underneath the gallery and immediately moved back from the balustrade. Someone was coming into the hall below. Max stood motionless in the darkest corner of the gallery and watched two men in white laboratory coats walk across to the center of the room. One of the men flicked a power switch, and for the next ten minutes they checked over and tested the electrical apparatus. Screens lit up, machines beeped, graphics and other data scrolled down monitors. The tests completed, the men sat down side by side at what looked like the main control console and waited.

Five minutes later, the door opened again and two armed guards entered the hall. Sandwiched between them was a man in handcuffs. At first Max wondered if it was the prisoner he'd seen being escorted from the motor launch that morning, but this man looked different. He was stripped to the waist and wearing nothing but a pair of white tracksuit bottoms.

The guards forced the man to sit in one of the dentist's chairs. They undid his handcuffs and strapped his wrists to the arms of the chair. Then they fastened his ankles down, too. Finally, they flipped out a couple of short metal arms from the headrest of the chair and clamped them into place around the man's skull. He was now almost completely immobilized. His eyes flicked around the room. He tried desperately to free his arms and legs, but they were secured too tightly. Even from this distance, Max could see that the man was terrified out of his wits.

The man screamed something Max didn't understand. It sounded like Arabic or some other Middle Eastern language. That made sense: He had dark skin and a close-cropped black beard. He shouted again, but the two men in white coats—the scientists or technicians—ignored him. They got up from their seats and attached a series of electrodes and wires to the man's body—one on either side of his head and several on his chest. Green lines pulsed across the bank of monitors, showing the man's heartbeat, blood pressure, and other bodily functions.

One of the scientists broke open a glass vial of colorless liquid and filled a hypodermic needle. Then he injected the liquid into the man's arm. For half a minute nothing happened, and then the man's eyes began to roll. His arm and shoulder muscles contracted and his whole body began to shake. Sweat broke out all over his chest, the droplets glistening on his skin. Then he arched his back violently and let out a piercing shriek of pain. Max turned away, unable to watch any more.

But as he turned, his left hand brushed against the wall, and the flashlight slipped from his grasp, falling to the floor with a clatter. The technicians and guards spun around and looked up at the gallery.

"It's the boy!" one of the guards shouted in Spanish.

Max scooped up the flashlight and darted back through the door into the office, and from there into the corridor. He guessed that the guards would probably come up the nearest staircase—the one to his left—so he sprinted the other way. He pictured Angel Romero's plan of the fortress in his head as he ran.

The building was basically a square with a courtyard in the middle and a staircase in each of the four corners. If Romero's memory was correct, there should be another staircase at the end of this corridor—and there it was. Max paused for a moment, but there was only one way he could realistically go. He bounded up the stairs two at a time. When he reached the third-floor landing, he kept going up. He was almost at the fourth floor when alarm bells went off all around the fortress. Every guard would be after him now. He needed somewhere to hide.

He turned along the landing and pushed open a door, praying that there was no one inside. There wasn't. It was a small room with a single bed in one corner and posters of supermodels on the walls. From the high, barred window Max guessed that this had once been a cell but had now been converted into living quarters for someone who worked in the fortress. A guard, perhaps? Max liked the irony of that. The guards were scouring the building for him and he was holed up in one of their rooms. He dropped to the floor and slid underneath the bed.

A few minutes later, the alarm bells stopped ringing. And ten minutes after that, Max heard a voice booming out from a loudspeaker in the courtyard, the words audible in every part of the fortress.

"Max? We know it's you, Max. Come on out." It was a man's voice, speaking in English with a soft American accent.

"Max," the man said again. "What's the point in hiding? We'll find you eventually, so why not save time and give yourself up now?"

Max stayed where he was. He wasn't turning himself in. Let them come and get him.

"Max, I have a friend of yours here. Say something to Max, Consuela."

Consuela's voice came over the loudspeaker. "Max, it's me." She sounded hesitant, nervous. "Max, don't trust them, they—" Her words were cut off abruptly. Then she screamed, a single cry of pain.

Max rolled out from under the bed and stood up, his fists clenching with anger.

"Did you hear that, Max?" the man said. "I don't want to hurt your friend, but I will if you don't come out now. Do you hear me?"

Consuela gave another cry of pain.

"It's up to you, Max," the voice continued. "Do you want Consuela to suffer? I'll give you three minutes to show yourself."

Max knew he had no choice. He couldn't stand by

and let them hurt Consuela. He had to surrender. From his pocket, he took the piece of wire he'd used to pick the lock in the cellars. He wound the wire around his finger a couple of times until it was the size of a wedding ring. He made sure there were no sharp ends sticking out, then put the wire in his mouth and swallowed it.

He opened the door. A window on the other side of the corridor overlooked the courtyard. Max saw a man in a black suit standing there with a microphone in his hand. Consuela was next to him, an armed guard on either side of her. She looked smaller and more vulnerable than Max had ever seen her. The man in the black suit glanced at his watch and raised the microphone to his mouth.

"You have two minutes, Max. Don't keep me waiting," he said.

Max went down the stairs and out through a door into the courtyard. Consuela saw him coming. She broke away from her guards and ran to him, throwing her arms around him and hugging him tightly.

"Don't worry about me," she whispered in his ear. "Save yourself, Max. You must get away."

The guards pulled them apart roughly. Max gave the man in the black suit a look of intense loathing.

"You sadistic creep," he said fiercely.

The man didn't take offense at the insult. He seemed almost amused by it. He turned to the soldiers. "Take the woman back to her cell and the boy to my office."

16

MAX LOOKED AROUND THE ROOM. IT WAS ON the ground floor of the fortress, a big corner office with a desk the size of a table-tennis table, a leather sofa and armchairs at one end, and a lot of artwork on the walls.

The soldiers had put him in a chair facing the desk and taken up positions beside him. When the man in the black suit entered the room, they stepped away from Max, but not far. Max was aware of them watching him, their submachine guns slung across their chests.

The man in the black suit sat in a high-backed swivel chair behind the desk. He was a nondescript person in almost every respect. He was neither tall nor short, fat nor thin. His hair was a mixture of brown and gray, his complexion was pinkish, and he wore rectangular rimless spectacles over pale-blue eyes that had as much warmth in them as an arctic lake. He was the kind of person you could pass in the street and not notice, or meet and forget about five minutes later. Yet Max realized he must be Julius Clark, the owner of Shadow Island and one of the richest men on earth.

"So you're Max Cassidy," Clark said. "You look like your father."

"You met my father?" asked Max.

"I saw his act at Playa d'Oro. He was very good. I understand you're quite an escape artist yourself." He smiled coldly. "Well, you won't escape from here. Do you know who I am?"

"You're a man who hurts defenseless women and tortures prisoners."

"So you saw our little experiment in the lab? You're wrong—that wasn't torture."

"It looked that way to me," Max said. "Why've you brought Consuela here? What do you want with her?"

"That doesn't concern you."

"I think it does. What is this place? Who are all the prisoners you're keeping here?"

Clark ignored Max's questions and asked one of his own. "How did you get onto the island?"

"I flew," Max replied.

"You're a bit of a smart aleck, aren't you? It doesn't matter. We'll get the answer out of you soon enough."

"What, you'll torture me too?"

"You should've kept away from here, Max. You should've let them send you back to England. You're just a kid."

"Maybe," Max said. "But I'm old enough to recognize a psycho when I see one."

Clark's mouth tightened. His icy blue eyes glared at Max. "You think I'm a psychopath?"

"You do a pretty good impression of one."

"You're a child, Max. A stupid, ignorant child. You have no idea what I am or what we're doing here." Clark nodded at the guards. "Search him. Thoroughly."

The soldiers hauled Max to his feet and went through his pockets. They found the screwdriver and held it up for Clark to see.

"Take your clothes off," Clark said.

"Get lost," Max retorted.

"Take them off, or my men will take them off for you."

Max shot him a hostile look, but he removed his

232

clothes, stripping down to his boxer shorts. He stood there almost naked, feeling exposed and humiliated, while the guards went through all his clothes, checking them for hidden tools.

"You escaped from the police station in Rio Verde," Clark said. "We're not as careless here. When we lock someone up, they *stay* locked up. Check his feet and hair."

The soldiers examined Max's toes and the soles of his feet, then combed through his hair.

"He's clean, Señor Clark," one of the men said.

"Take away his belt and wristwatch," Clark ordered. Then, to Max, "Put your clothes back on."

"My father came here, didn't he?" Max said. "What happened to him?"

Clark didn't answer. He waited until Max was fully dressed, then waved a hand at the guards. "Put him in a cell."

"What are you going to do with me?" Max asked.

"You want to know what we do here," Clark replied. "You're going to find out."

The cell was on the third floor of the fortress. It was about the same size as the one in the police station, only the floor was stone flags and there was a proper bed, metal framed, bolted to the floor, with a thin mattress, blanket, and pillow on it. A rusty metal bucket in the corner must have served as a toilet.

Max paced restlessly around the room, cursing himself for dropping his flashlight on the gallery. That had been stupid, unforgivably careless, and now he was paying the price.

At least he hadn't been put in one of those tiny black holes in the cellars. That was something to be thankful for. His cell had a window of sorts, a small square opening with no glass and three thick steel bars cemented into the stonework around it. If he stood on the bed, he was just tall enough to see through. He was on the outside of the east wing of the fortress, with a view over the sea. He gripped hold of the bars and shook them. They were fixed firmly into the walls. Not that this made any difference. Even if there'd been no bars over the window, it wouldn't have provided an escape route. There was nothing outside except a sheer hundred-thirty-foot drop to the rocks below.

Max had other ideas about how he was going to get out. And he had every intention of doing so. He wasn't going to wait for those men in white coats to strap him into that chair and pump him full of chemicals. Julius Clark had sneered at him, called him a stupid, ignorant child. Well, he'd show them what a "child" could do.

He went to the middle of the cell and stretched out his arms and shoulders, standing up as straight as he could. Then he closed his eyes and concentrated on working the muscles of his abdomen and alimentary canal. The ring of wire would still be down there in his stomach. It shouldn't be too hard to bring it back up. He felt a slight flutter just below his rib cage and knew that the valve at the top of his stomach was opening, the muscles around it expelling the circle of wire. Slowly, the wire came up past his tonsils and into his mouth.

He pulled it out and unrolled it. It was a crude implement, but he'd studied the door lock carefully when the guards had brought him in. It was old, probably dating back to the 1970s. The piece of wire should be enough to pick it.

But not yet. He had to make himself wait. There might still be guards outside. He'd let things settle down before he went to work on the door.

He lay on the bed and tried to relax a little, but it wasn't easy. He was impatient to get going on the lock. *Give it five or ten minutes,* he said to himself. He attempted to distract himself by thinking about the other people who had been kept prisoner here before him. *What terrible hardships did they suffer?* he wondered. He thought about the pirates who'd lived on the island four hundred years earlier, and then the political prisoners who'd been locked away by the generals—men like Angel Romero and Luis Lopez-Vega. How many of those prisoners had died on Shadow Island? Did their ghosts still haunt the stairs and passages of the fortress?

"Is there somebody there?"

Max stiffened. Had he imagined the voice?

It came again. "Hello?"

A man's voice with an English accent, calling faintly from somewhere.

Max sat up and looked around. The cell was in darkness. There was a bulb high up in the ceiling, but the guards had switched it off from outside after they'd locked Max in. "Who's that?" he called.

Was the voice outside in the corridor? Max got off the bed and crouched by the door, peering through the keyhole. "Where are you?"

"Over here," the man said.

Max spun around. "Where?"

"In the corner."

Max went to the far corner of the cell.

"Low down," the voice said.

Max felt the wall with his hands. At the very bottom was a crack where the mortar had broken away from between the stones. He knelt down beside it. He could feel a slight draft coming through the gap, but he couldn't see anything.

"Are you next door? In a cell too?" the voice asked.

"Yeah."

"Where are we?"

"Shadow Island."

"Never heard of it."

"It's off the coast of Santo Domingo."

"Santo Domingo? In Central America?"

"Yes."

"You sound like a boy."

"I am, I'm fourteen," Max said.

"*Fourteen!* Jesus, they've got kids here too? What's your name?"

"Max Cassidy."

"Nice to meet you, Max. I'm Chris Moncrieffe. I'd shake hands, only it's not exactly possible at the moment. You English?"

"Yes."

"Me too. How long've you been here?"

"Just a few hours."

"I only got here today as well."

"Are you the man in the blue shirt and handcuffs I saw arriving by boat?" Max asked.

"Yeah, that was me. They've taken the handcuffs off now, thank God."

Max leaned back against the wall. Talking to this stranger in the adjoining cell made him feel better, gave him something to focus his attention on while he waited for the right moment to tackle the door. He liked the sound of Chris Moncrieffe's voice. There was something reassuring about it.

"You know anything about this place?" Chris asked.

"It's an old Spanish fortress," Max replied. "Owned by a businessman named Julius Clark. Why've they brought you here?"

"That's a good question. I have no idea."

"Really? You must have done something."

"I guess I was just in the wrong place at the wrong time."

"What do you mean? What place, what time?"

"The Amazon rainforest. That's where I was when I was abducted."

"You were kidnapped?" Max said.

"I can't see any other way of putting it."

"Who by?"

"A company named Rescomin International. You heard of them?"

"No."

"They're a multinational corporation, very big, fingers in all sorts of pies—minerals, commodities, timber. That's why I was in the Amazon. I was working for an environmental charity named Rainforest Watch. They needed a researcher with jungle experience. I was in the army for ten years, spent plenty of time in the jungle—Borneo, Central America, Brazil. Rainforest Watch wanted someone who knew how to survive out there for long periods. And that's where I've been for most of the past year, surveying the forest, keeping tabs on Rescomin. Rainforest Watch suspected they were illegally chopping down trees and selling the hardwood on the international market."

"And were they?" Max asked.

"That's exactly what they were doing. Clearing huge areas of forest and shipping out the timber. I watched them for weeks, living undercover in the jungle, taking photographs, making notes about their operations. Then I got careless. I went too close to one of their logging camps. A company security guard caught me. They confiscated my reports and camera and locked me up in a shed for a couple of days. Next thing I

239

know, they handcuff and blindfold me, put me on a plane, and fly me out of the Amazon. I was kept in a cellar somewhere for a few days, then flown somewhere else, transferred to a boat, and here I am—on 'Shadow Island,' apparently."

Max was silent for a few seconds. He was taking in everything Chris had told him. "I can't believe a multinational corporation could do that kind of thing to someone."

"Well, they did. Crazy, isn't it? They're stripping the Amazon rainforest of trees, probably paying the authorities to turn a blind eye to what they're up to. They're destroying the environment and making a lot of money out of it. And I'm the one who ends up locked in a cell. What makes me even more angry is that I had photos, notes, a ton of evidence to prove they were logging illegally, and now that's all gone." Chris gave a long sigh. "But that's enough about me. How about you? What's a fourteen-year-old boy doing here?"

Max told him. Chris listened to his story, mostly in silence, though he laughed when Max described escaping from the police station in the back of the car.

When Max had finished, Chris said, "You're one gutsy kid, aren't you? You reckon your dad did come here? That he was kept a prisoner like us?"

240

"I don't know," said Max. "But I'm going to find out."

"Have you seen much of the island? You think we have any chance of escaping?"

"It won't be easy. There are a lot of guards—Julius Clark seems to have some kind of private army—and they're all carrying guns."

"Could we swim for it—if we can get out of the fortress?"

"The currents are supposed to be dangerous. But I'd be willing to give it a go."

"Count me in too," Chris said. "Of course, we have to get out of these cells first. You have any ideas about that?"

"Give me a minute," Max said.

"What?"

"We'll talk again in a minute."

Max went to his cell door and listened. He'd waited long enough now. He could hear no sounds of a guard outside. Inserting his piece of wire into the keyhole, he went to work on the lock. One by one the tumblers clicked back. Max pulled open the door and looked out. The corridor was deserted.

In two strides, he was at the door of the adjoining cell, picking the lock. He threw back the door and stepped inside. Chris Moncrieffe was still sitting on the floor in the corner of the cell, his knees drawn up to his chest.

"I'm sorry," Max said. "It took me a bit longer than a minute."

Chris gaped at him. "What the . . . ? How in God's name did you do that?"

Max held up the wire. "It's easy when you know how."

Chris scrambled to his feet. He was a tall, muscular man with a tanned face, short black hair, and dark stubble along his jaw line. He held out a hand. His grip was firm and unyielding.

"Not bad, Max, not bad at all," he said dryly. "What now?"

"We rescue Consuela, find out anything we can about my dad, then get the hell out of here," Max told him.

17

"DO YOU KNOW WHERE SHE'S BEING KEPT?" Chris asked, pausing for a second as they went out into the corridor.

"No," Max replied. "I just know she's somewhere in the fortress."

"We'll have to check all the cells then."

Chris moved off along the wall. He stopped by the first door he came to and flipped down the small metal hatch that was used for delivering food and water to any prisoner held inside. It was too dark to see whether the cell was occupied. "You see a light switch anywhere?"

"Here," Max said. His fingers found a switch on

the wall and clicked it on.

"Empty," Chris said, peering around the interior of the cell. "You check the next one. We'd better move fast. Someone may notice the lights going on and off."

Max went to the adjoining cell and snapped open the hatch with one hand while his other went to the light switch. That cell was empty too.

Chris had moved farther down the corridor and was squinting through another hatch. "What does Consuela look like?" he said.

"Dark, slim, beautiful," Max replied.

Chris flashed a grin at him. "Just my type."

They checked all the cells along the corridor. None of them was occupied.

"You know where the other rooms are?" asked Chris.

"The floor below, I think," Max said. "But there may be guards."

"Leave them to me," Chris said.

His self-assurance boosted Max's own confidence. He was no longer entirely on his own. Chris was a soldier, a man who seemed to know how to take care of himself.

They padded down the stairs to the third floor, Chris

leading the way. He moved softly and dangerously, like a stalking leopard. On the landing at the bottom of the stairs, he stopped and put out a hand, warning Max to keep back.

"There's someone there," Chris whispered in Max's ear.

They pressed their bodies to the wall. Max could hear the faint scuff of boots around the corner. The sound drew nearer, louder. A guard emerged on the landing. He wore khaki fatigues and a peaked cap; a submachine gun dangled from one shoulder.

Chris moved swiftly. He stepped out behind the man and hooked an arm around his neck. The guard gave a low choking cough and collapsed to the floor, unconscious. His weapon hit the stone tiles with a clatter.

"Damn," Chris breathed. "Let's hope no one heard that."

He picked up the submachine gun and Max followed him along the corridor, pulling open the hatches in the doors.

In one cell Max saw a man lying on a bed—the Arabic-looking man he'd watched being strapped into the dentist's chair and given the injection. The man sat bolt upright, as if he were having a nightmare, and started to scream, his eyes bulging in terror, saliva foaming at the corners of his mouth.

"They'll hear that, though," Max said. "Quick, check the other cells."

They sprinted along the corridor, taking alternate doors. Every cell was empty.

"What now?" Chris said. "Where else do we look?"

"I don't know," Max said. "Consuela could be any-where in the building."

The man was still screaming. Max knew it would only be a matter of minutes before a guard came to see what was going on.

"We can't hang around here," Chris said. "Which way do we go?"

"It doesn't matter," Max said.

Two soldiers appeared at the far end of the corri-dor. They shouted out in Spanish and fumbled for their guns.

"Well, that narrows our choices a little," Chris said.

He turned and ran for the nearest stairwell. "Up or down?" he said.

"Up," Max decided.

They raced up the stairs. There were footsteps above them, loud, urgent footsteps that echoed about the stairwell. A figure came around the corner and almost collided with Max. It was another guard. He stopped, a cry of shock bursting from his mouth. Chris took full advantage of his surprise. He grabbed hold of the man and threw him down the stairs.

More guards came into view below them. Chris fired a burst from the submachine gun. The men dived back out of sight.

"I'll handle them," Chris said. "You get away."

"But that's not—" Max began.

"Now!" Chris snapped. "I'll give you time."

He fired another burst, then looked hard at Max. "You know my story. Contact Rainforest Watch—tell them what happened to me."

Max sprinted up the stairs. On the third-floor landing he paused. He heard gunfire below. Two quick bursts followed by silence. Was Chris still alive? Max's heart was thumping, blood pounding inside his head. He imagined Chris lying dead on the floor, the soldiers trampling over his body and climbing the stairs after him.

His chances of escape were slim. Max knew that. But which way to go? More guards would be on their way now. They'd quickly seal off all the staircases, the corridors, then close the net on him. He couldn't afford to delay. He ran up the next flight of stairs and out through a door onto the roof of the fortress.

To his intense relief, he saw that there were no sentries up here. But it wouldn't remain that way for long. He looked around desperately for somewhere to run or somewhere to hide. For an instant, he wondered about jumping, before dismissing the idea as suicidal. On one side of the battlements was a sheer drop to the courtyard. On the other he saw only rocks at the base of the cliff.

He ran toward the northeast corner of the roof, keeping well away from the inner parapet so he wouldn't be spotted from the courtyard below. He could see no obvious place to hide, and just running around the roof made no sense at all—he'd simply end up back where he started. There had to be another way off it. There *had* to be.

He glanced over the battlements. Nothing there, just a smooth stone wall. Could he climb down it? Not a chance. There were no foot- or handholds. He checked again a few yards farther on. Still the smooth wall with nothing to hang on to. He reached the corner and took another look over the battlements.

There was a terrace right below him, outside one of the rooms on the fourth floor of the fortress. It was a long drop, but Max could see no other way of escape.

He climbed over the battlements and lowered himself down, hanging by his arms, his body flat against the wall of the building. As he was hanging there, he heard the door from the stairs bang open. Pulling himself up a few inches, he looked back across the roof. Two armed guards were standing by the door, gazing around, arguing about something, though Max was too far away to hear what they were saying. Did they know he'd come up here? Maybe not. No one had actually seen him go all the way up to the roof. For all these men knew, he might have stopped on the fourth floor and hidden in one of the rooms there. They could see Max wasn't on the roof. With any luck, they would just go back down and continue their search for him inside the fortress.

But no, they weren't going back down. They split up, taking a side of the roof each, examining the walls, peering over the battlements. Max knew he had to move now. He dropped so that his arms were fully extended and then let go. As his feet hit the terrace, he bent his knees and rolled onto his side to break his fall. Then he scrambled up, pulled open the door into the building, and darted through it.

The room inside was small, only six to nine feet square, and sparsely furnished. There was a table against one wall and a cupboard in the corner, but nothing else. The floor, like the rest of the fortress, was made from stone slabs.

Max moved across the room. The door in the far wall, he guessed, gave access to the corridor, but there was also a second, internal door. He tried that first. It was heavy metal, about four inches thick. It opened into a darkened room, but there was enough light trickling in from the windows for him to see that it was much bigger than the first one. And much cooler. Strangely cool, in fact. It wasn't a natural kind of temperature, the sort of chill you often got in old stone buildings at night. It was artificial. Max could feel cold air circulating, hear a low background hum of machinery. That explained the insulated door. He was in some kind of refrigerated cold storage.

But what was stored here? Max could detect a strong, unpleasant smell but couldn't identify what it was. Was it rotten food? He could see no sign of boxes or cartons that might contain foodstuff. The walls of the room were blank. There were no cupboards or shelves. All Max could see was three tables lined up across the center of the room. At least, he thought they were tables. When he moved closer to inspect them, he saw that they were actually trolleys with wheels—like the beds they used in hospitals for moving patients around.

On each of the trolleys was an object—something bulky, nearly six feet long and a foot and a half wide. Max touched one. It was encased in a zip-up black plastic bag and felt soft under his fingers. He shivered. He was beginning to suspect what the objects were.

He located the zip and tugged it down. The unpleasant smell suddenly grew stronger. The black bag gaped open and Max saw a face inside—a man's face. He could just make out the features. The eyes staring up at him, the mouth contorted into a grimace of pain. However this man had died, it had not been a peaceful end.

Max zipped the bag closed again and stepped away from the trolley, feeling breathless, slightly sick. He didn't want to go near the other two body bags, but he had to know what they contained. He unzipped each of them in turn. There were dead bodies inside both. One was a fat, middle-aged man with a beard, the other a much smaller guy who looked only a few years older than Max. Like the first corpse, these two had faces that were frozen into masks of pain and fear.

What is going on here on Shadow Island? Max wondered. A "little experiment," Julius Clark had called it. What had he meant by that? What kind of experiment?

Were they trying out new drugs on the prisoners? Whatever had killed these three men, it hadn't been natural causes.

Max heard the click of a door opening. He went rigid.

A light snapped on in the adjoining room. Someone was coming.

Max looked around, trying not to panic. There was just the one door into the room, no other exit except the windows—and they were too high to jump from. Nor was there any furniture he could use to conceal himself. There was only one place he could hide. He shuddered at the thought, but didn't hesitate for long. He unzipped the body bag on the third trolley and quickly slid inside it, shifting the corpse over to make room. He pulled the zipper shut and lay still, trying not to gag at the foul smell.

The cold-storage door opened. Someone came in. More than one person. Max heard two sets of footsteps. No, three. Three people had entered. The light came on.

"Jeez, this place is starting to stink," a man's voice said in English. "How long have these bodies been here?"

"Two days, I think, señor," another man replied.

"Have the technicians finished with them?"

"Yes, señor."

"Then what're you waiting for? Get rid of them."

"Now, señor?"

"Yeah, now. Before I throw up."

One set of footsteps left the room. The two people who'd remained behind had a short conversation in Spanish, then the trolley underneath Max vibrated and began to move. It was being wheeled out of the room.

The body bag shifted slightly as the trolley turned to negotiate the doorway. Max rolled against the corpse beside him and his cheek touched the face of the dead man. The skin felt cold and clammy. Max resisted the urge to pull away in disgust. He clenched his teeth to stop himself retching and kept motionless, his body pressed against the corpse so that from outside it would appear as if there were only one person inside the bag.

They went out onto the terrace, the trolley wheels rattling over the stone walkway. Max felt someone fiddling with the end of the body bag, attaching something to it; then the bag was lifted off the trolley. Max hoped that no one would notice the extra weight. The dead man next to him was only slightly built, as was

Max. The two of them together would probably only weigh the same as a big man.

The body bag swung back and forth a couple of times, then Max felt himself being thrown out into space and falling.

18

DOWN AND DOWN HE PLUMMETED. MAX could hear the air whistling past the bag as it fell. He was terrified, knowing he might be dead in seconds. He braced himself automatically for the impact that was to come. If it was solid ground, it was all over. If it was water, he had a chance of survival.

It was water. The bag hit the surface of the sea with a force that was like a hammer blow to the body. Max had tensed all his muscles in readiness, but even so the wind was knocked out of him. For a moment he couldn't breathe; then he gasped in a mouthful of air just a split second before the bag submerged and began to sink. Water poured in through the opening by the zip, flooding over Max's face. He reached up, his hands searching for the tag. The bag was sinking fast. They must have tied weights to it to make sure it didn't float back up. The water was all around him now. He couldn't see. The corpse beside him was pressing against him, crushing his chest. He didn't have much air in his lungs. There hadn't been time to gulp in enough. Where *was* the zip? It was somewhere here. It had to be. The bag was still sinking. How deep were they going? Max thought suddenly of his act— his escape from a sack in a freezing-cold water tank. If he could do that, then he could do this.

His fingers found the tag. He pulled hard on it. The zip didn't budge. He pulled again. His lungs were ready to burst. The zip moved a couple of inches, then jammed. Max tugged on it. It didn't move. He slid both hands into the narrow opening and grabbed hold of the sides of the bag, wrenching them apart with all his strength. The zip came loose and the bag split open. Max got his shoulders out through the opening, then the rest of his body. The bag kept sinking, falling into the murky depths. Max took a last look at it, then kicked toward the surface.

It was a long way up. So long that he thought he wasn't going to make it. There was nothing left in his lungs. His heart, his muscles were working on determination and grit alone. Max didn't believe in defeat.

He saw a shimmer of light above him and found a new surge of energy. He was nearly there. He broke the surface and gulped in the sweet night air.

He was in a small cove. There were high cliffs on two sides; on the third, the walls of the fortress rose up from a base of massive rocks. The terrace from which he'd been thrown protruded out over the cove, enabling objects to be dumped directly into deep water. Max wondered how many bodies there were down below him at the bottom of the ocean.

He was tired. His earlier swim through the sewage pipe, his escape from the cell, and now his submersion in the body bag had combined to exhaust him. He needed to rest. He swam to the rocks at the foot of the fortress and dragged himself out of the water.

For twenty minutes or more he lay on the rocks, getting his strength back. Then he noticed the sky was getting lighter. Dawn was approaching. If he wanted to find a way back into the fortress, he would have to act now, while he still had the cover of darkness. And he was determined to get back in. He had to save Consuela. If he didn't, they'd strap her into that horrific chair and inject her with chemicals. Max couldn't let that happen to her.

Getting wearily to his feet, he examined his surroundings. The cove was almost a complete circle, a narrow gap at one side giving access to the open sea. The cliffs were steep. If there was no alternative, he'd probably be able to climb them, but Max thought he could see an easier way out. The rocks immediately below the fortress walls had a much shallower gradient. There was a cave in the center, and from there the rocks were stacked one on top of the other to form a series of steps and platforms. Some of the steps were high, but Max reckoned there'd be plenty of hand- and footholds to help him get up them.

He clambered across the lowest tier of rocks, which, from the thick covering of seaweed and pools of salt water, were clearly submerged at high tide, and over a lip into the cave. He peered into the blackness. The cave only had a small opening, but it seemed to go back a long way. Max went farther inside, picking his way over the slippery pebble-strewn floor. At one side, high up near the roof, he saw a narrow fissure in the rock. If he could get through that, he could climb onto the outcrop at the right of the cave and begin his ascent to the fortress. But first he had to reach the fissure.

He ran his hands over the wall of rock and found

a couple of cracks to hang on to, then a foothold. He pulled himself up, locating more clefts and ledges to assist him. Within a short time he had climbed twelve feet and was almost touching the roof.

It was then that he saw the glint of something shiny in the shadows at the back of the cave. An hour earlier he wouldn't have noticed it—it would have been too dark. But now it was just light enough for him to make out a metallic line on the surface of the rock. He moved sideways along a ledge to take a closer look. There was a thin iron rail embedded in the wall and, below the rail, a series of steps that were too even and uniform to be natural. They had to be manmade.

Strange, Max thought. *Steps? Why would someone have cut steps into the rock?* Then he remembered something that Angel Romero had mentioned—about the pirates who'd used Shadow Island as their base in the sixteenth century digging tunnels to give them an escape route from the fortress. Was that what this was—the end of a tunnel?

Max took hold of the iron railing and went carefully up the steps, feeling his way more than seeing it. There was a natural chimney at the back of the cave through which the steps ascended, then a narrow passage that had been hewn out of the rock by hand. It had been cleverly done: At intervals there were boreholes in the side of the passage to allow light to shine through here and there. With the sun already creeping over the horizon, faint glimmers were trickling in, enabling Max to see where he was going.

At one point the passage widened out into a small natural chamber that had a fault line in the roof, allowing even more light in; then it shrank back to a tunnel so low that Max had to stoop to get through.

He'd climbed sixty feet or more, he estimated, when the tunnel came to an abrupt end. It was pitch dark again here, so he couldn't see the wall in front of him, but he could feel that it wasn't a natural slab of rock. There were regular horizontal and vertical joints in the surface where squared-off stones had been cemented together.

Had the pirates' escape route been blocked off sometime in the four hundred years since they'd abandoned the island? Or was this wall an integral part of the route? Max explored with his fingers. It was about the width and height of a standard door. But *was* it a door?

He pushed with his hands. It was as solid and immovable as the rock around it. Max pushed in a different place—on the left-hand side. Still nothing moved. He tried the right and this time felt the stones give a little.

He pushed again, harder. He hadn't imagined it. The stones had definitely moved a fraction. If it was really a door, it probably hadn't been opened for centuries. The mechanism would be stiff. He put his shoulder to the stones and applied all the pressure he could muster. He heard a creak, like a rusty hinge, and the wall suddenly jolted back a couple of inches. Max felt round the edge. There was the beginning of an opening. He pushed with his shoulder again, using all his weight. Very slowly, the wall of stone swung inward to reveal a doorway in the rock.

Max stepped through. Light now filtered through an iron grille on the wall above his head. He was back in the cellars of the fortress. The room was similar to the one he'd entered from the sewage outlet—a high-vaulted chamber with bare stone walls and a stone floor. Max paused to rest for a moment. He was tired, but he knew he had to keep going. He was back inside the fortress. That was risky, but he had to find Consuela, and he had to discover whether his father had come here, and what had happened to him afterward.

Max went to the door. It wasn't locked. He stepped into the corridor and paused, picturing the layout of the fortress in his mind again. He was on the north side of the building. Where was Consuela being held? He'd have to work his way through the rest of the rooms until he found her, but there was another job he had to do first.

He moved cautiously along the corridor and then up the stairs. Would the guards still be searching the fortress for him? They'd had more than enough time to go through all the rooms, so maybe the search would have been moved outside the fortress.

On the ground floor he stopped again. The floodlights were still on in the central courtyard, but Max could see no sign of any guards. He flitted along the corridor to Julius Clark's office and tried the door. It was locked, but Max still had the piece of wire in his pocket. In just a few seconds he had the door open. There were windows on both the north and west walls of the room. Through the west window, Max could see the mainland, the lights of Rio Verde twinkling on the hillside, the outlines of the buildings emerging from shadow as the sun rose. In the channel near the mouth of the river, Julius Clark's massive yacht was clearly visible.

Max went over to the desk. The drawers were locked, but the locks were no match for Max's skill with a wire hook. He pulled open the top drawer. It contained envelopes and other stationery—and a gleaming silver automatic pistol. Max lifted it out. He'd never handled a gun before and he was surprised by how heavy it was. He put the weapon down on the desk and went through the other drawers. Most contained nothing of interest—a diary, more stationery, a ball of string, staples, and other office supplies. But one drawer was filled to the brim with money, crisp new U.S. thousand-dollar bills bound together in half-inch-thick packets. Max stared at the cash. There had to be more than a million dollars in the drawer.

But it wasn't money he'd come for. He turned his attention to the metal filing cabinets behind the desk. They contained folders, arranged in alphabetical order, each one labeled with what appeared to be a man's name. Some names looked English, others were clearly foreign. *James Abbott, Sergei Alekseev, Narang Anwar, Redmond Ashworth-Ames, Erik Blomkvist.* Max flicked through the folders, noting the dates on the covers, and stopped abruptly, staring at the name on one of the files. His mouth had gone suddenly dry. His hands were shaking. Yes, it was there: a file marked *Alexander Cassidy.*

Max put it on the desk and opened it. There wasn't much inside, just a few sheets of paper. On the first sheet were personal details. His father's name and place and date of birth. Then there were his postal address and email address, his cell and landline phone numbers, National Insurance number, and other bits of information such as height, weight, eye color, and blood type. Underneath these details was a note that read, *Date of admission—8 June 2007.*

Max gazed at the words, feeling his heart miss a beat: 8 June 2007. That was the day after his father had disappeared, the day after he had supposedly been murdered by Max's mother. Here was confirmation that Helen Cassidy could not possibly have killed her husband and that he had been brought to Shadow Island. But why had he been brought here? What was Julius Clark's interest in him? Were there things about his dad that Max didn't know? Important things?

The file gave no answer to these questions. It said nothing else about his stay on the island. The remaining three sheets of paper looked like printouts of medical tests. The top line of text on the first sheet read, *9 June, 11:25 hrs—5ml Episuderon,* and below that were rows of figures and readings that seemed to relate to bodily functions such as heart rate, brainwaves, blood pressure, and respiration.

Max couldn't understand what the figures meant, but he could guess where they'd come from. Episuderon, that had to be a drug. His father, like the man Max had seen in the laboratory, had been injected with the drug, and these printouts recorded how his body had reacted to it.

It appeared that Alexander had only been given that one injection. What had happened after that? Had the injection killed him? Was his body down at the bottom of the cove with all the other corpses? If it was, there was no record of it in this file.

Max removed the sheets of paper, folded them up, and slipped them into his pocket. He was returning the folder to the cabinet when he heard a noise behind him. He spun around to see Julius Clark entering the office.

19

CLARK STOPPED DEAD, GAPING IN ASTONISH-ment at Max. Then he lunged toward the desk.

Max was too quick for him. He snatched up the pistol and pointed it at Clark. "Get back!"

Max held the gun tightly with both hands. He didn't want Clark to see how much he was trembling. "Get back, or I'll shoot."

Clark backed away, raising his hands. "Don't be stupid, Max," he said. "Where's this going to get you? Put the gun down and let's talk."

"We'll talk," snapped Max. "But I'm not putting the gun down. I've just found my father's file. He came here the day after he disappeared. You kidnapped him, didn't you? Then you framed my mother for his murder with the help of the local police. Why?"

"You're just a kid, Max—" Clark began.

"Don't give me that crap," Max broke in angrily. "Just answer my questions. What's Episuderon? Why did you bring my father here? What did you do to him?"

"Sometimes people have to be sacrificed for the common good," Clark said.

"What's that supposed to mean?"

Clark shrugged. "It means that some things are bigger, and more important, than a single person's life. You're young, Max."

"Stop telling me I'm young."

"You have no idea how the world really works. How complex it is, how so many things are linked together. You don't understand how dangerous a place the world can be, how many people out there would like to destroy it."

"What are you talking about?"

Clark's pale eyes glinted like chips of ice. There was something very hard about them, something calculating and ruthless. Max felt a sharp stab of fear in his stomach.

"We have to protect ourselves, Max. That's all we're

doing here. We're trying to protect the world from dangerous fanatics."

"You're saying my father was a dangerous fanatic? You're mad."

"Am I?"

"And what about Consuela? What about Chris Moncrieffe? Are they both dangerous fanatics too?"

"Fanatics come in many shapes and sizes," Clark said. "Some are easy to identify; with others it's much harder, but they're there all the same. That woman working behind the counter in your local grocery store, that man driving a bus, that old guy digging his vegetable patch. They may not look dangerous, but how can you be sure? How can you be sure what they're thinking, what they're planning? That's all we're trying to do. Find out who the dangerous fanatics are so we can deal with them."

"'Deal with them'?" Max said. "You mean *kill* them?"

"Killing is not part of our plan."

"You're lying. I've seen the bodies in that refrigerated cold storage."

"My, you have been getting around the place, haven't you? They were accidents."

"And my father—was he an accident too? Or Luis

Lopez-Vega? You killed him, didn't you?"

"Max, this isn't—"

"*Didn't you?*"

Clark shrugged. "Yes, I had Lopez-Vega killed. He was a troublemaker. He had to be removed."

"And the fisherman, Fernando Gonzales? His death wasn't an accident, was it? You killed him and made it look as if he'd drowned."

"Gonzales was unfortunate," Clark said. "He brought your father out to the island on his boat. Your father went snooping where he shouldn't have been snooping. Gonzales knew too much. We couldn't afford to let him live."

"And my dad? You kidnapped him and brought him back here. You injected him with Episuderon. Why? What harm had he ever done you?"

Clark's mouth twitched in a faint smile. "We know so little about our parents, don't we? We forget that they had lives before we were born. We never think that they might still have secret lives that we know nothing about."

"Secret lives? My dad didn't have a secret life."

"Oh yes, Max, he did. His stage act was just a cover, a legitimate reason for him to travel around the world doing other things."

"What other things?"

"You don't know? I'm not surprised. Your father was a careful man. That's why it took us so long to catch him."

"What things?"

"Put down the gun, Max. You can't get away from here. There are armed guards all over the fortress. You're on an island. The Santo Domingo police and armed forces—the whole government in fact—are in my pocket. It's five thousand miles to England. Do you really think you have a chance of escaping?"

Clark took a step nearer.

"Get back!" Max ordered.

"Or what?"

"Or I'll shoot you."

Clark gazed at him, studying his face, his eyes, the pistol gripped in his hands. Then he laughed, a manic, high-pitched laugh that made Max's flesh creep. "I don't think so, Max. I don't think you're going to shoot me."

"Don't push me," Max said.

"It takes a certain type of person to be able to kill another, particularly in cold blood. You're not like that." Clark took another step toward him.

"Get back, I said!" Max snapped.

Clark kept coming.

"Do you hear me? Stop right there."

"Shoot me if you want," Clark said. "Go on."

Max knew that Clark was right. He wasn't a killer. He couldn't shoot anyone. He backed away.

"I mean it, I'll shoot you," he said, aiming the pistol at Clark's head, but even Max knew he didn't sound convincing.

Clark went for him. There was a brief moment when Max could have pulled the trigger, but he didn't. Clark grabbed the gun and tried to pull it away. Max hung on, refusing to let go. Clark lashed out with his fists, hitting Max on the jaw. He reeled backward but kept hold of the pistol. Furious now, Clark swung another punch. Max twisted nimbly out of the way and Clark overbalanced, tumbling sideways and catching his head on the corner of the desk as he fell. He lay on the floor, unconscious.

Max was breathing heavily, massaging his jaw where he'd been hit. He looked down at Clark's body. He could leave him where he was, but he didn't know how long he'd remain unconscious. It might only be a few minutes. Max needed longer than that to find Consuela. He pulled open one of the desk drawers and took out the ball of string he'd noticed earlier. He rolled Clark over onto his stomach and tied his hands together behind his back. Then he bound his legs together and tied them to the desk. Rummaging in Clark's suit pockets, he found a handkerchief, which he crumpled up and stuffed into Clark's mouth, gagging him, wrapping more string around his face to hold it in place. It was a crude piece of work, but Max knew a lot about knots and bonds. Clark wouldn't be able to free himself without help.

Max opened the desk drawer containing the money and looked at the packets of thousand-dollar bills. A plan of escape—not just from Shadow Island, but from Santo Domingo as well—was beginning to form in his mind. And the plan required money, possibly a large amount of money. He lifted out two packets and riffled through the cash. He guessed there were about fifty bills in each packet. That was fifty thousand dollars, a hundred thousand in total. That was more than enough. He stuffed a packet into each of his pockets, picked up the pistol, and opened the office door.

The corridor outside was deserted. Max headed for the east side of the building, the gun ready in his hand. It was still useful as a threat. As he reached the end of the corridor, where it made a ninety-degree turn to the right, he stopped and risked a look around the corner.

He caught a fleeting glimpse of a man being escorted through the door to the laboratory. Max couldn't see the man's face, but he was wearing jeans and a blue shirt.

Was it Chris Moncrieffe? Surely not. He was dead, wasn't he? Max waited a few seconds, then ran to the laboratory door. He pushed it open a fraction and slipped quietly through. Just inside the door was a bench with a stainless-steel top covered with bits of scientific apparatus. Max ducked down behind it and looked across the room. A guard was standing to one side while the two men in white coats strapped the prisoner into the high-tech metal chair in the center of the laboratory. When the men moved out of the way, Max saw that it was indeed Chris. Somehow, he was still alive. Then Max saw something that sent a chill up his spine. The second metal chair was also occupied—by Consuela.

She was strapped down, with electrodes attached to her head and body. Had she already been given an injection? Max thought not. She seemed calm but alert. He was just in time.

The white-coated men were checking their monitors now. Max had a pistol. He could deal with them. But what about the armed guard waiting patiently on the sidelines? Was he going to go, or stay to watch the next stage? He was going to stay, Max decided. One of the scientists picked up a hypodermic needle and a glass vial of liquid. Max knew he had to do something fast. He dropped to the floor and snaked round the room, always keeping out of sight beneath the benches.

When he stood up again, he was only a yard or so behind the soldier. The scientist was next to Consuela, about to plunge the hypodermic needle into her arm. Max stepped forward and put the barrel of his pistol to the back of the soldier's head.

"Drop your gun!" he shouted.

The man started and began to turn. Max jabbed his pistol hard into his skull. "Now!"

The guard slid the submachine gun off his shoulder and let it fall to the floor. The men in white coats were staring open-mouthed at Max.

"Move back," he ordered. "And keep your hands in the air." Then, to the guard, he said, "Take three paces forward."

Max bent down and picked up the submachine gun. One of the scientists made a move for an alarm button on the control console. Max aimed his pistol at the console and fired. The recoil was much greater than he'd expected. The bullet went high, shattering one of the computer screens. The scientist froze.

"You move again and I'll shoot *you*," Max said. "Understand?"

He circled around, his pistol covering the men. He stopped behind one of the chairs and unstrapped Chris.

Chris stood up and took the submachine gun from Max, leaving him with the pistol. "That's what I like about you, kid," he said. "Your sense of timing."

Max released Consuela from the other chair.

"You okay?" he asked, helping her up.

She nodded and hugged him tightly.

"Thank God you're all right," she said.

"Someone will have heard the gunshot," Chris said. "We shouldn't hang around."

He pointed the gun at the guard and the two scientists. "Over there," he commanded, indicating a door in the corner of the laboratory.

He herded the three men toward it at gunpoint. It led to a small storeroom. Chris forced the men inside and locked the door behind them.

"I thought you were dead," Max said to Chris.

"Not yet," he replied. "But there's still time," he added, as three soldiers burst through the door at the far end of the room.

"Get down!" Chris yelled to Max and Consuela,

before firing a short burst at the soldiers.

The guards fired back, but by now Max and Consuela and Chris himself were flat on the floor behind one of the benches. Chris lifted the gun over his head and fired blindly in the direction of the soldiers.

They retaliated with a barrage of bullets. Computer screens shattered, glass jars of chemicals smashed, and the air was filled with clouds of noxious fumes. Then one of the broken monitors short-circuited, sending out a shower of sparks. There was a sudden whoosh as these ignited the fumes, then a huge explosion that reverberated around the laboratory, sending debris flying across the room. Flames leaped into the air, licking the wood-paneled walls and ornate ceiling. Clouds of thick smoke ballooned out as the whole laboratory turned into an inferno.

"Let's go!" Chris said, getting to his feet and running for the nearest exit.

Max and Consuela went after him. The room was well ablaze by now, the wall of smoke screening them from the guards.

Chris whipped open the door and looked out, ducking back in quickly as he saw three more guards at the far end of the corridor. They were heading for the door at the other side of the laboratory. Chris waited for them to disappear from view, then darted out and sprinted in the opposite direction, Max and Consuela following.

"How do we get out of here?" Chris called over his shoulder.

"Go left at the corner," Max shouted back.

They raced down the corridor, turned into the north wing of the fortress and kept going. As they reached the northwest corner, Max suddenly stopped.

"Wait!" he cried.

Chris turned. "What's the matter?"

"The other prisoner upstairs. We can't leave him."

"You mean the guy who was screaming? Why would you—?"

"We have to get him out," Max said.

"Look, kid, that's not a good idea."

"They'll kill him if we don't."

Chris opened his mouth to argue, but Max was already running up the stairs.

"Is he always this stubborn?" Chris said to Consuela.

"He has his moments," she replied, then turned and chased after Max.

Chris came up the stairs behind her and they followed Max to the third floor and along the corridor toward the cells. They could smell the smoke from the fire downstairs.

"This whole place is going to go up in flames," Chris

277

said. "We'd better hurry. Which cell was he in?"

"This one, I think."

Max flipped down the hatch in one of the doors. The prisoner was still inside, lying on his bed. He was awake, but tossing and turning from side to side, foaming at the mouth.

"What the hell have they done to him?" Chris said. "Stand back."

He shot the lock away with his gun and kicked in the door. The man stared at them with terrified eyes. He let out a piercing scream, shaking his head to and fro, then backed away into the corner.

"We're friends," Max said. "You understand? Friends, okay?"

"Just grab him," Chris said. "We're wasting time."

He slung the weapon over his shoulder and seized the man by the arms, hauling him up from the bed. Max and Consuela took one side, Chris the other, and between them they half dragged, half carried him out of the cell. The stink of smoke was getting stronger. Black clouds poured out across the courtyard.

The man was limp in their arms now, offering no resistance. He was muttering to himself, repeating the same thing over and over. "Friends, okay. Friends, okay."

"He's lost his mind," Chris said. "He's finished.

What're we going to do with him?"

"Get him help," Max said.

They carried the prisoner along the passage and down the stairs. The fire had spread from the east wing. The ground floor was filled with choking fumes. The smoke was so thick that visibility was down to only a couple of yards.

"Where now?" Chris said hurriedly.

"The main entrance is that way, near the southwest corner," said Max.

"Are there guards?"

"I think so."

"We could try to shoot our way out."

"There are too many of them," Max said.

"Look out!" Consuela yelled.

A soldier had erupted from the fog of smoke. Chris let go of the prisoner, reaching for his submachine gun, but he was a moment too late. The guard fired, hitting the prisoner in the chest. Chris fired back. The guard flung himself sideways through an opening into the central courtyard.

Max and Consuela kept hold of the prisoner and dragged him into the nearest room—the fortress kitchens. Chris let off another burst of machine-gun fire to keep the guard at bay and dived in behind them. He tipped over a large cupboard to barricade the door.

Max and Consuela lowered the prisoner gently to the floor. There was blood all over his chest and more seeping from his mouth.

"What do we do?" Max asked desperately.

"I don't know," Consuela replied. "He's badly hurt."

"There's nothing we can do," Chris said.

"There must be. How do we stop the bleeding?"

"It's too late for that."

Max was still holding the man's hand. He looked up at Max, his face screwed up with pain. *"Arhat Zebari,"* he whispered. *"Arhat Zebari."* Then he died.

Max stared down at his lifeless face, feeling a shiver run through him. He'd never seen a man die before, never felt such a chilling sense of despair. Who was this wretched prisoner? Why was he on Shadow Island?

Consuela put an arm around Max and pulled him close. "He's gone," she murmured softly.

"We have to get out. Save ourselves," Chris said.

He went to the window and peered out. It was only a short drop to the ground outside. "We should head for the jetty," he said. "There's a boat there. Max? *Max!*"

Max tore his gaze away from the dead man. "What?"

"You and Consuela get out the window."

"Window . . ."

"Now. Do you hear me? I'm going to create a

diversion, give them something to keep them busy."

Chris went down the line of stoves, turning on all the burners. The room filled with the foul smell of propane gas.

"Max, we have to go," Consuela said urgently.

She pulled him to his feet and they scrambled through the window. Chris followed a few seconds later. He was holding a kitchen cloth and a box of matches.

"Take cover behind those rocks," he said.

He set fire to the cloth and tossed it back through the window, then hurled himself to the ground as an enormous explosion ripped through the kitchens. The stone walls were solid enough to withstand the force, but the windows were blown right out. Sheets of roaring fire erupted through the openings, the flames scorching the outside of the building.

The three of them got to their feet and ran along by the fortress walls to the jetty. There were two patrol launches tied up. An unarmed sailor was standing on the deck of the first boat, staring at the smoke pouring from the fortress.

"Off the boat!" Chris shouted at him. "Who else is on board?"

Another sailor and the boat's skipper emerged from the cabin. Chris fired into the air above their heads as a warning. "Move!" he yelled at them.

The men clambered quickly out onto the jetty.

Chris aimed at the hull of the second launch and let off another burst of machine-gun fire, putting holes in the boat below the waterline. Within seconds the launch started to list to one side.

"Look!" Consuela cried. She pointed back toward the fortress, where the big main doors had been opened. Armed soldiers were streaming out and running down the steps toward the jetty.

Chris leaped on board the first patrol boat. Max untied the stern mooring rope, Consuela the bow; then they jumped down onto the deck. The guards were nearly at the jetty now, only fifty yards away. Chris turned the ignition key and the patrol boat's engine kicked into life. The soldiers were running along the jetty. They raised their guns.

"Chris!" Max shouted, pulling Consuela down into the shelter of the cabin.

Chris rammed the throttle lever forward and threw himself to the floor, just as a hail of bullets cut through the wheelhouse, shattering the windows. The patrol boat surged away from the jetty, the sea foaming violently in its wake. The guards fired again, but the boat was fast getting out of range.

Max craned his head up and looked back. The

soldiers were standing in a group at the end of the jetty. Behind them, the fortress was blazing like a beacon, flames leaping from the windows, creeping across the roof so that the whole building was enveloped in fire and smoke.

20

CHRIS GOT UP AND TOOK THE WHEEL OF THE boat, adjusting their course to take them north along the coast. He kept the throttle on full so the launch was touching thirty-five knots.

Max and Consuela came out from the cabin and joined him in the wheelhouse.

"You okay?" Chris asked.

Max nodded. Consuela looked at him, her expression concerned. "Are you sure? What happened back there . . . seeing that poor man . . . it was awful."

"I'll be all right," he said.

He felt numb, slightly sick. The prisoner's death had shaken him. "What did he mean?" he said. "*Arhat*

Zebari? Was that his name?"

Consuela came over and gave him a hug. "Try not to think about him, Max. You did all you could."

"Hey, what about me? Don't I get a hug too?" Chris said, grinning at Consuela.

Consuela eyed him coolly. "I don't even know who you are."

"Chris Moncrieffe. Pleased to meet you." He held out his hand.

Consuela hesitated, then shook it. "Where are we going?" she asked.

"As far away from that island as we can get," Chris replied.

Max turned and looked back. The fortress was burning fiercely, the fire out of control. Great clouds of black smoke were billowing up into the sky.

"They're going to come after us," he said.

"How? We took the only usable boat," Chris pointed out.

"There are boats on the mainland. And Julius Clark has a helicopter on his yacht."

"We'll worry about that when it happens," Chris said.

"I think it already is," Consuela told him. She was gazing across to the mainland. A boat was heading out toward them from the mouth of the Rio Verde.

"That's just some clapped-out old fishing boat," Chris said dismissively. "We can easily outrun it."

"No," Max said. "Slow down."

"What?"

"Throttle back."

"Are you out of your mind?"

Max waved at the other boat. "I know who it is," he said. "Change course to meet it."

"You sure?"

"I'm sure."

Chris pulled back the throttle lever and turned the wheel. The *Rosario* came alongside them and Isabella stepped out of the wheelhouse.

"I was waiting by the shore. I see the fire," she called across to them. "Are you all right? Do you need any help?"

"Can we come on board?" Max called back.

"Of course."

"What're you doing?" Chris protested. "This launch is much faster, much better equipped than that piece of junk."

"It's also the boat that everyone will be looking for," Max replied. "Julius Clark's people, the Santo Domingan navy, if there is one. This is the boat they'll come after."

"You've got a point," Chris conceded. "But we can't just leave it here so close to the mainland. They'll know we've transferred to some other vessel."

"Can we point it out to sea and just let it go?" Max suggested.

"Leave it to me. You two get off," Chris said.

Max and Consuela climbed over the side of the launch onto the deck of the *Rosario*. Chris maneuvered the patrol launch around until it was facing due east. He found a piece of rope in a locker and lashed the wheel to the control panel, so that the rudder wouldn't move. Then he opened up the throttle. The launch sped away. Chris ran to the side and dived over. By the time he'd swum to the *Rosario* and clambered aboard, the patrol boat was half a mile away, heading toward the horizon.

"Which way we go?" Isabella asked.

"North," Max replied. "Away from the island and Rio Verde."

Isabella swung the wheel over, and the *Rosario* turned and headed up the coast.

Chris stripped off his dripping wet jeans and shirt. "You got any spare clothes on board?" he asked Isabella.

"In locker," she replied. "There are old clothes—work

clothes—of my father. He use when he repair boat."

"They'll do," Chris said, pulling out a pair of oily trousers and a threadbare shirt. "Now let's see where we are."

He lifted down a maritime chart from a shelf and spread it out. "You're the guy with all the ideas," he said to Max. "What do you suggest? Do we put into a cove somewhere and lie low? Or do we keep going, try to get to a neighboring country?"

Max glanced at the chart. It was large scale and very detailed. Every navigation buoy, every tiny island, every submerged rock was shown on it. He took a closer look and felt his heart give a jolt. He'd just noticed something around the edges of the chart—numbers and lines dividing it into small grids. *Is it possible?* he wondered.

He counted off the squares along the side and top of the chart and put his finger on a spot—a headland in the north of Santo Domingo.

"That's where we're going," he said.

Isabella steered the *Rosario* as far into the bay as she dared, then cut the engine and threw the anchor overboard. The bay was small and isolated, with a shingle beach and a low, rocky headland at the north end. The beach was deserted, the land behind it covered in trees and dense vegetation. There were no houses or other signs of human habitation.

Max took the two packets of money from his trouser pockets and placed them on the dashboard. The others stared at the bills in amazement.

"Where did you get those?" Consuela asked.

"Let's just say it was a gift from Julius Clark," Max replied.

He turned to Isabella. "How much did your father earn in a year?"

"My father? I don't know. In good year, maybe a thousand dollars."

Max peeled off ten of the thousand-dollar bills and held them out. "Take them. That's ten years' income. Enough to support you and your brothers and sisters until you start earning money yourselves."

"For me?" Isabella said. "Why?"

"Call it compensation. Your father was murdered by Julius Clark's men. Clark admitted it to me."

Isabella's face turned pale with shock. "Why? Why would Señor Clark kill my father?"

"Because he knew something Clark wanted kept secret. That day your father took my dad out, they didn't go fishing. They went to Shadow Island. My dad was up to something—I don't know what. He went snooping on the island, and your father was murdered to prevent him talking about it."

Chris picked up the remaining bills. "That's a lot of money. What're you going to do with it all?"

"Get home for a start," Max said. "We can't fly back to England from Santo Domingo now. We'll need to get to Nicaragua, Honduras, or Belize, one of those places, and buy new air tickets, pay for new passports. Money will be useful."

He picked up the maritime chart and walked onto the deck. He went to the side of the boat and swung his leg over the rail.

"We won't be long," he said to Isabella.

"Wait a minute," Consuela said. "Where are we going?"

"To solve a puzzle, I hope," Max said. He jumped down into the shallow water and waded ashore.

Consuela and Chris exchanged looks, then Chris shrugged. "Why not?" he said. "He seems to know what he's doing."

Chris vaulted over the rail into the sea, then turned to offer Consuela a helping hand.

"I can manage," she said stiffly. She lowered herself over the side and followed them onto the beach. "What puzzle?" she asked Max.

"You remember those numbers I told you about?

That I found on the piece of paper under Luis Lopez-Vega's wig? They weren't a code or the combination to a safe. I think they were a grid reference. A grid reference here in Santo Domingo."

Max opened the chart on the beach and pinned down the corners with pebbles.

"One-one-one-three—that's eleven degrees and thirteen minutes north. Then eight-three-five-two. That's eighty-three degrees and fifty-two minutes west. Where those two lines intersect is right here, on the headland."

"Why would Lopez-Vega have wanted to give you a grid reference?" Consuela said.

"There's only one way to find out," Max replied.

He folded the chart up again and walked along the beach, the shingle crunching beneath his feet. At the north end of the bay, he scrambled onto the headland and waited for Consuela and Chris to join him.

"If I'm right," Max said, "the exact point should be about thirty or forty yards along the headland. Somewhere . . ." He screwed up his eyes against the glare of the sun. "Look, what's that?"

He climbed over the rocks and out along a rough, sandy track.

On a small patch of earth, well above the tide line, someone had built a low cairn—a mound of stones like the ones hikers use to mark footpaths in the mountains.

Max knelt down and took it apart, stone by stone. The mound was hollow, and in the center was a small package wrapped in plastic to protect it from the weather. Max unwrapped the bundle. Inside was a folded piece of paper. He stopped breathing for an instant. There was a name written on it—*Max*.

With trembling fingers, he unfolded the letter. He recognized his father's handwriting immediately, though some of the words were shaky and blurred, as if Alex had had trouble holding his pen steady.

The letter was dated just a fortnight earlier. Max stared at the words. He was in a daze, disbelief and excitement coursing through him. His father had written this a mere fourteen days ago.

He was alive.

Dear Max,

I don't know if you will ever read this letter. I don't know if Luis Lopez-Vega has managed to find you. But I am writing it as a precaution, in case Luis has failed in his mission or in case something happens to me.

Please forgive me for not getting in

touch with you sooner, but I have not been well for a long time. Is it really two years? I find it hard to believe. I am still not completely better. There are days, like today, when I can think clearly, but there are other days when my mind seems to go blank and I cannot remember anything. It is the effects of the drug they gave me on Shadow Island.

I did not know your mother was in prison until Luis Lopez-Vega told me just a few days ago. When you see her, tell her that I am thinking of her always. She must be patient a little longer. Her suffering will soon be over.

I would like nothing better than to see you both again—I miss you terribly—but that reunion must wait awhile. I am a hunted man, and I fear that if I surface too soon, I will be killed. Or worse, that you and your mother will be harmed. I cannot let that happen—you are both too precious to me. I cannot risk putting either of you in danger. I have work to do that means I must go away for a time—I do not dare say too much here in case this letter falls into the wrong hands. You must be careful, Max. You are a clever, resourceful boy, but the forces ranged against us are powerful and ruthless. They will try to destroy you, as they are trying to destroy me, and as they are trying to destroy the earth with their greed. But the Cedar Alliance is strong. It has the conscience of the world on its side, and I truly believe that good will triumph over evil.

Have courage, Max. And have hope. We will all be together again soon.

Trust in me.

With all my love,
Dad

Max gazed at the words on the page. His whole body was quivering, his pulse racing, his vision blurring. He was breathless, faint with shock and joy.

Consuela gently took the letter from him. She read through it, her eyes lighting up, then filling with tears. She put her arms around Max and held him tight. "I thought he was gone," she whispered, her voice choking with emotion. "Oh, Max, I'm so happy." She pulled away and smiled at him.

Max took the letter back and clutched it in his hand. He stared out across the ocean. There was a lump in his throat, tears in his eyes. After two long, unbearable years, he'd heard from his father. But where was he? What did his letter mean? What powerful forces was he talking about? Why did he have to go away again? What was the Cedar Alliance? More questions. So many questions for which Max had no answers.

"I trust you, Dad," Max said softly, the tears running down his cheeks now. "But I'm not going to wait another two years to see you. I'm not going to wait another two years before Mum gets out of prison. I'm coming to look for you. I don't care how dangerous it is. And I promise you one thing—I'm going to find you."

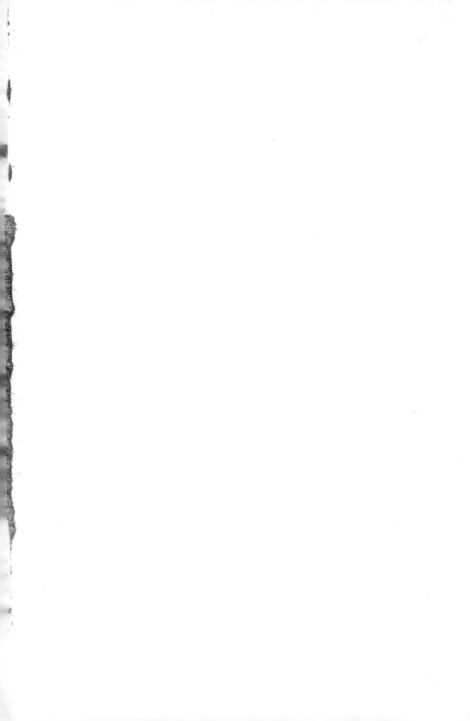